AF431884

THE SHANGHAI HORROR

ARBOGAST

THE BIZARCHIVES

INTRODUCTION

In the golden era of fiction before grand cinema, before video games and even before comic books. There was one form of entertainment so widespread, so prolific, that it could be found in every break room and bathroom. The mighty pulps. Some called them dime novels or magazines but these publications predated magazines. They were part magazine, part comic, part literature and all excitement. Pulp fiction was the go-to entertainment for the American working class. From this epoch, everything good in today's pop culture was born. You can't play a single game, read a book or see a film that doesn't have pulp DNA.

Everything we know about horror, action, romance, adventure, fantasy and science fiction was born out of this period. And boy did the pulps have plenty of it. And today the genres born from pulp wonder stories are well represented among us underground pulp publishers. We at The Bizarchives love our cosmic horror, weird sci-fi and brutal sword and sorcery tales. But we're not alone. Several other publishers like us do an excellent job of printing stories with far flung galaxies and medieval high adventure. However, the early pulps contained one genre that gets slightly overlooked these days. And that's the hardboiled detective tale.

Hard knuckle gumshoes getting to the bottom of their cases with nothing more than quick wit, a sharp tongue and a mean pair of fists. Snubnose revolver carrying noir tough guys who haunt the city streets looking for clues as they rough up petty miscreants.

In The Shanghai horror, prolific modern pulpster Arbogast delivers us a tale that belongs in the pulpy pages of the 1930's. But, in typical Bizarchives fashion, he melds it with the spooky elements we all love. Cults, demons, bizarre rituals and he sets it all in the mysterious far east. Enjoy yourself as he takes you back in time to a bygone era where men were men and the weird was weird. Action, adventure and intrigue await you in the sultry streets of old Shanghai.

Enjoy,

• Dave Martel, The Bizarchives editor-in-chief

The Bizarchives

Weird Tales of Monsters, Magic, and Machines

Presented by

The Midgard Institute
of Science Fiction & Fantasy Literature

This work would not have been possible without the help of The Bizarchives, especially the Editor-in-Chief, Dave Martel. Thank you for the bottom of my bowels, kind sir.

Thank you also to all the contributors to The Bizarchives, as well as to my fellow SubStack scribbler, The Pulp Archivist. You have inspired me more than you know.

CONTENTS

CHAPTER 1
A CHANCE ENCOUNTER

"I DON'T KNOW about you, but I'm starting to get bored," Bergstrom said while sipping on his sixth beer of the day. He did not appear tipsy. Kenaghan knew from experience that it required a shipload of booze to get the Swede drunk. The straw-colored lager in Bergstrom's glass mirrored his light blond hair. His languid blue eyes were hooded with drowsiness. Despite coming from the same race that produced the Vikings, Bergstrom was a fan of doing as little as possible each day.

"Yeah, I think you're right," such laconic responses were the norm for Kenaghan. He had been nicknamed "The Spartan" in the Foreign Legion for a reason. He kept his comments short and sweet, plus he lived cheaply and ate sparsely. Bergstrom, on the other hand, was a big spender. The Swede loved to dine on big, juicy steaks and glasses of red wine. The men made an odd pairing, but there was a synergy to their relationship—Kenaghan provided the muscle and experience, while Bergstrom's spending habits gave Kenaghan a reason to ply his trade.

. . .

Kenaghan was also the opposite in terms of looks, as the American had dark hair and eyes. While Swede was tall and thin with the hands of an artist, Kenaghan was short, stocky, and sported hands so calloused that it was impossible distinguish between blisters and digits.

On that day, while sitting in Bergstrom's apartment in the International Settlement, both men needed work and, more importantly, excitement.

"I know a Chinese bookie who is always hiring security. Are you interested?"

"No."

"There's always Sweden. My family has connections to Bofors. We could make a lot of money selling guns and artillery to the Soviets."

"You know how I feel about the Reds."

"Sure, but don't you like green?" Bergstrom laughed at his little joke. Kenaghan remained stoic.

"You're just being a typically thick-headed mick. There's plenty of money to be made around here. I'll wager that if we wait long enough, there will be another war soon."

"Ok. Which side should we join?"

"Whichever one pays the most," Bergstrom said.

"You know how the Chinese are. Can never count on being paid on time or in legitimate currency."

"That is why we force their hands," Bergstrom stood up and showed Kenaghan his open palms. The American disliked his friend's theatricality, as he found it unduly effeminate. But, true to his nature, Kenaghan kept his comments to himself.

"Leave it to me, old friend. I will make sure that we find something and find it soon. In fact, I'll offer you a wager." Kenaghan showed no interest in the offer, but Bergstrom went ahead anyway. "I'll bet you a thousand dollars that I can find something fun, dangerous, and, most importantly, lucrative before the clock reaches midnight tonight. Do we have a deal?"

Kenaghan said nothing. Instead, he stood up and shook his friend's hand. The gesture produced a smile on the Swede's lips. The smiled was oily and impish, just like Bergstrom.

"It's settled then," he said. "I will see you at twelve sharp tonight at the Jade Dragon."

With the appointment set, Kenaghan grabbed his hat and coat and walked out into the gloom of a Shanghai afternoon. Thoughts poured through his mind as he walked the streets. He knew about the Jade Dragon's infamous reputation. It was a den of thieves—a favorite hangout for whores, gunrunners, and warlords cooling their heels between campaigns. If Bergstrom planned to rendezvous at the Jade Dragon, then Kenaghan knew that something illegal or violent awaited him. A normal man would have seen the bad news brewing and backed out. But Kenaghan had stopped being normal over a decade ago, and fate, history, and honor made it impossible for him to leave Bergstrom in the lurch.

Against the backdrop of chattering Chinese speaking in Mandarin, Cantonese, and the various sub-dialects of both, and while occasionally stopping to enjoy the smells of hotpot stands or *xiaolongbao* sellers, Kenaghan took a moment to appreciate the long and strange journey his life had taken. All signs and augurs would have predicted a hum-drum life for the kid from the Susquehanna Valley. Instead, a few tragic events and a chance encounter had put Kenaghan on a twisted path that led all the way to Cathay.

. . .

Kenaghan's father came from Ulster. As much as he had tried to leave the sectarian feuds of his homeland behind, the old man could not escape them entirely. Because of creed, he was locked out and barred from working in the mines by Irish labor unions distrustful of men from the north. He got far more than rejections; Kenaghan remembered seeing a note held in place on the family's front door by a blade. Kenaghan was too young to read the words or understand the situation at the time, but his father's rejection let him, a boy barely old enough to walk, realize that the world could be a dangerous place.

His father did find work in the end, but most of his jobs ended after a month or two. The old man took to drink to heal his spiritual wounds. When the demons grew too loud and could not be silenced with whisky, the old man would strike Kenaghan's mother. She, a hardened girl born and raised on the tobacco farms of Maryland, never complained about her rough treatment. Instead, she followed her husband's lead and beat the ever-loving beejeezus out of her son. The kids at school called Kenaghan "Glasses" because of how often he showed up to class with two black eyes. The teasing and name-calling did nothing more than make it easier for Kenaghan to drop out in the seventh grade.

Of course, Kenaghan did not leave school on his own accord. His parents needed extra money and help around the house, and both agreed that schooling was an extravagance. Kenaghan was first put to work in the fields for a kindly farmer named Blackledge, and then found steady and but no less burdensome work with the Vulcan Iron Works in Wilkes-Barre. Kenaghan hated every minute of it. The only benefit was that it allowed him to spend most of his day away from home, where his drunken father and increasingly angry mother bickered nonstop.

· · ·

On Saturday nights and Sunday mornings, Kenaghan also found relief in the arms of prostitutes. The thick-hipped German girls and their thinner Connecticut Yankee co-workers would listen to him bellyache for a few coins. That's all Kenaghan had wanted; the rest was an extra bonus.

By the time he turned seventeen, Kenaghan came to a brutal realization: his future looked like nothing more and nothing less than working like a dog six days a week with occasional flesh and barleycorn for relief. The thought repulsed him. Something primordial in him demanded action—demanded the courage to take a stand for a life worth living. So, at seventeen, Kenaghan traveled by himself to Scranton and found an Army recruiter willing to take him.

It did not take long for Kenaghan to learn to hate the Army. He hated all the regulations, all rules, and all the sergeants. He hated the dumb privates he was forced to share bunks with, and he hated the smart ones who lorded their high school diplomas over him. He hated everything except the guns. He found that he loved to shoot. Better yet, he had a natural aptitude for handling rifles, revolvers, and shotguns. He earned all the top marksmanship awards in his division, and as such the Army found it appropriate to give him some time with the machine gun companies. He excelled there too. The only problem was that it was peacetime, so Kenaghan got to shoot at targets and nothing more. He put in requests for the Philippines, but they all got denied. Like his old man before him, Kenaghan found solace in the bottle. He earned a reputation at Fort Riley for being a sullen, obstreperous ox who would fight anyone at any time. Few soldiers took Kenaghan up on his challenges. The unlucky handful who did learned to regret it, as the Pennsylvania iron worker could break bones and tear muscle without so much as breaking a sweat.

. . .

Everyone on base was relieved when April 1917 came around, Kenaghan chief of all. The Pennsylvania private oiled his Enfield twice on the night before their train journey across the country to New York City. He counted his bullets several times over, savoring every bit of their lethal capacity. While the other men enjoyed the smuggled liquor on the train ride east, Kenaghan kept to himself and his weapon. He watched the flat prairies of Kansas become the hills of Kentucky. He got a glimpse of New York City for the first time and felt next to nothing. The big city's skyscrapers bored him, and he was annoyed by how giddy the other men were about Broadway and Wall Street. What limited horizons, Kenaghan thought; better to be focused on killing the enemy and the adventure of blood guts awaiting them in France.

The killing had to wait, for, even in France, the Army found a way to ruin Kenaghan's expectations. Rather than be sent to the frontlines right away, Kenaghan's unit stayed behind the lines for a month for additional training. They were put under the care of a sergeant from the 1st Infantry Division, plus they got added instruction on infiltration and machine gun tactics from a French officer who spoke through an interpreter. Kenaghan started plotting his escape the minute the Frenchman gave him a Chauchat. Kenaghan fired a short burst before chucking the light machine gun in a ditch.

"What a piece junk. Between that and a spear, I'd prefer to do my fighting with a spear." For his impetuous display, Kenaghan was put on extra rations and held back from training. That meant that when the division finally did go to the front, Kenaghan would still be in the rear waiting to join a new unit just beginning their own training. Spending his war in the rear was not an option that Kenaghan was willing to except. So Kenaghan did the only thing he could—he deserted.

. . .

One night, well after lights out, Kenaghan snuck out of his tent and slipped past the sentry on duty. Two camps over were the "Blue Spaders" of the 26th. Scuttlebutt at the time said that Roosevelt's regiment was headed for Cantigny as part of a major counterattack against the Germans. Kenaghan found their camp and slept in the woods rather than risk finding a spot in a tent. When reveille sounded, Kenaghan found his place in muster.

"Jones!"

"Here," Kenaghan had said to the company sergeant.

"You don't look like Alfred Jones, private."

"I'm not Alfred Jones; I'm Luke Jones, sergeant."

"I don't have a 'Luke Jones' on my roster."

"I got separated from the 28th yesterday. Hoofed it back here so I could link up and fight another day, sergeant."

The sergeant looked hard at Kenaghan. "You abandoned your brothers in the heat of combat, private? That's called desertion."

"No, sergeant. I got separated. Besides, it is better to be here where I can do some more fighting with the 26th than stew in Flanders as a POW." Kenaghan's words had an immediate effect on the sergeant. The hard-looking bulldog nodded and returned to his roster.

"Ok, boys. Say hello to Luke Jones. You might want to watch what he does, because unlike you lot, he's already seen battle." The men around Kenaghan looked him over. Some scowled, while others greeted him. The lie had worked; now it was up to Kenaghan to prove his worth in combat.

The 26th marched out of camp that morning. By mid-day they reached a vulnerable spot in the American line at Cantigny. The sergeant, whose name was Galloway, told the men that their mission was to reduce the salient in the American line. As a group, the men of the 26th realized that they were in for real fighting. Kenaghan attached his bayonet without prompting; the other men followed suit. They all believed that the deserter was in fact a veteran rather than just a good liar.

Ten minutes after five o'clock, the 26th was ordered to attack. The deafening roar of artillery guns and the staccato burst of German machine guns began and never ceased. Kenaghan watched men fall all around him—some died with visible wounds on their foreheads and chests, while others fell and never revealed their scars. All died with their eyes open and mouths wide. Some appeared to be dancers frozen mid-waltz.

Kenaghan pushed forward. He was terrified. He felt like a failure because of his fear. His trembling hands caused him to miss his first five shots. Upon reloading his Enfield, he dropped his five-round stripper clip in the mud.

"Dammit! Get a grip man," he said to himself.

"Hey! I thought you were the tough one. You seem pretty spooked to me." The voice belonged to a skinny and pale private from the 26th. Kenaghan bared his teeth and growled at the kid.

"The enemy is the Hun, not me."

Incensed, Kenaghan grabbed his third stripper clip, reloaded his Enfield, rejoined the fight. The first day of the counterattack was a blur of movement and noise. Kenaghan remained on the run for hours, stopping occasionally to take shots at the enemy. The men of the 26th fought like lions that day, including men who outshined Kenaghan by magnitudes.

· · ·

This fact made him dangerously morose. He stewed for hours in his foxhole. He chastised himself for cowardice and for letting himself down. He grumbled that he had failed to kill a single man despite firing more times than he could count.

"Not a bad first fight, eh?" The skinny and pale private plopped down beside Kenaghan. In his hand was a clear glass bottle with a thin trace of amber liquid at the bottom. "Would you like a pull?" he asked.

"Why have you been bothering me all day?" Kenaghan growled.

"They told me that you were a first-rate fighter. They said it would be wise to shadow you. Boy, they were wrong."

"Shut your mouth!"

"Tough talk from a weak man." That was it—the final straw. All of Kenaghan's disappointment and rage came out of him in that moment. He pounced on the other man like a tiger going after prey. He placed his thumbs on the man's windpipe before using them to scratch his victim's eyes. The man called for mercy, but Kenaghan kept beating him with his fists. Eventually, the other man stopped moving.

Realizing what he had done, Kenaghan removed all the man's ammunition, removed his ID tags, and dragged his body closer to no man's land. Kenaghan prayed that the private's body would get pulverized in the next barrage, but he did not wait around to see if God would answer his prayers. Kenaghan deserted for the second time, and rather than find another Army unit to join, he beat a trail for the next safe French village. After several nights of starvation and thirst, a wet and muddy Kenaghan arrived in a no-name village in the Somme where no one spoke English.

· · ·

He wisely discarded his uniform after mugging a drunken peasant out for a twilight stroll. The peasant's clothing gave Kenaghan a level of protection as he eventually made his way to the coast. There, Kenaghan found more illusory safety—a bustling port city where sailors, deserters, criminals, and whores commingled on the streets.

Kenaghan's original goal was to find a ship going anywhere. Instead, one night while sleeping in the same flophouse with other undesirables, Kenaghan was roused by gendarmes. The French police screamed at him in their tongue. One officer, a fat slug with a thin mustache, kicked Kenaghan several times in the stomach while calling him dirty names. When Kenaghan went to take a swing, another officer hit him with a truncheon. The blow made Kenaghan dizzy before ultimately sending him into unconsciousness.

As bad as the Army had been, it was nothing compared to a French prison. Endless days of moldy bread and thin beef stew kept Kenaghan and the other men alive but miserable in every other respect. When they weren't eating, they were kept in their cramped cells and denied sunlight. The guards hoped to starve the prisoners into submission. At night, just before they were forced to listen to the rats and cockroaches scuttle across the floors, a recruiting sergeant would come around and ask them to sign a piece of paper. Kenaghan eventually learned from a Belgian who spoke English that the sergeant was looking for volunteers for the Foreign Legion. If the men signed, then they would be let out of prison, given better food, and given pay.

"Why does nobody sign the paper, then?" Kenaghan had asked the Belgian.

"Most of the people in here are anarchists. They hate the army, and they hate the war. They would rather starve then serve the republic."

"Nuts to that," Kenaghan said. He got the ear of the recruiting sergeant and signed the man's paper that night. Kenaghan was yanked from his cell and put on a motor to the frontline. He was officially a member of the famous Foreign Legion. They gave him an old French rifle, new blouse and trousers, and wished him luck.

Kenaghan spent several months at the front. Unlike the US Army, the Foreign Legion was well-versed in deserters. Every corporal made it his business to harass their men every night to make sure they were still there. Kenaghan learned to love the daily grind of combat. Each patrol saw his nerves lessen a little bit until, by war's end in 1918, Kenaghan was a battle-hardened veteran respected by his fellow dregs in the Legion. The Spartan had finally found a home.

Rather than go back to the iron works, or worse the US Army, where he would have been sent to Leavenworth for life, Kenaghan made a home in the Foreign Legion. He saw action against Arabs in Algeria and Morocco, and, in his final year, he was posted to Indochina. Kenaghan found the East a sensual playground, and, better yet, a place far enough away from his past that he could remake himself. That is exactly what he did: Kenaghan spent a summer in Saigon and worked for a Chinese loan shark. The loan shark put in a good word for Kenaghan with the Green Gang in Shanghai. Months later the American found himself in the crown city of the East. He was put up with other foreigners in the International Settlement. The Green Gang kept him on a retainer for whenever they needed something done among the whites. It was good money, but not enough for Kenaghan. That's how he came to know Bergstrom. The rich kid from Stockholm was the International Settlement's gadfly and the go-to source for easy money. To his surprise, Kenaghan grew to like Bergstrom even after spending so many nights with him beating up welchers or running down unproductive sing-song girls.

The thought of Bergstrom brought Kenaghan back to the present moment. He looked at his wristwatch and realized that he had been walking the streets for hours. He had enough time left for a meal before the Jade Dragon, so he went to a familiar haunt. The place did not have a name or even a sign, but every foreigner in the French Concession knew about Mama Anh and her hand-pulled noodles. Kenaghan applied the secret knock (two short taps followed by four long pulls) and was let into what was essentially the elderly chef's kitchen. The kitchen was empty at that time of night, so Kenaghan got his steamy bowl of noodles in minutes. The noodles were delivered to him by a sweet-looking waitress who moonlighted as a chorus girl. Kenaghan recognized her after a while. She seemed to recognize him straight away but stayed coy. Kenaghan flashed a rare smile into between slurps as he pondered the differences between men and women when it came to post-intimacy relations.

Kenaghan left his bowl on the table and made his way to the Jade Dragon. He found the inside of the bar covered in the smoke of a hundred cigarettes and pipes. One of the cigarettes belonged to Bergstrom, who waved Kenaghan over to a table near a far corner. Seated at the table was another whom Kenaghan had never seen before. His expression was sharp and rigid, and his hair had exact dimensions. The monocle over his right eye, plus the brown leather gloves on his hands, let Kenaghan know right away that he was a military officer of some kind.

"This is our new friend Colonel von Oppersdorff. He's with the German mission to the Nationalists," Bergstrom said. The stiff-necked Prussian officer bowed slightly at the waist.

"Nice to meet you," Kenaghan said.

"Go ahead, colonel. Tell him the plan. I have already heard it, but I would love to hear it again."

. . .

"Well," the colonel began in his strong German accent, "as Herr Bergstrom has already said, I am with the German government's mission to the National Revolutionary Army. Currently I am on leave. I am scheduled to go back to Canton in a few days, and I would like to bring you men along with me."

"Why?" Kenaghan asked. Bergstrom used a small hand gesture to try and remind Kenaghan to be on his best behavior.

"How much do you know about the German government's mission in China, Herr Kenaghan?"

"All I know is that you guys train the Nationalist army that wants to take over all of China. The warlords in the north, and their Japanese backers, have other ideas."

"That is true on a general level but allow me to elucidate a few facts. First, while I do represent the *Reichswehr* in an official capacity, and while I do spend my days trying to teach barbaric bandits and peasants how to be proper soldiers, neither of these things are my main mission. Rather, my main mission lies in Germany. Namely, the overthrow of the illegitimate Weimar government and constitution and the restoration of Kaiser Wilhelm II."

"I fought against you and your emperor not too long ago," Kenaghan said while lightning his own cigarette. "Bergstrom here sat out the war, didn't you?" Bergstrom was forced to conceded with a sheepish smile.

"My country was neutral," he said.

"I bear no ill will towards you, Herr Kenaghan. I am sure you fought honorably, as I fought honorably too. Besides, the squabbling of white men means little in Asia, where we are surrounded on all sides by a civilization that seeks to colonize us. Do not let the smiling coolies or comely wenches fool you."

"Never have and never will."

"*Sehr gut.*"

"But what about business, colonel?" Bergstrom said.

"Ah, yes. Business is the primary function of manhood. You are both men, so I will not waste your time anymore. Herr Kenaghan, I want you and Herr Bergstrom to pose as fellow German officers. Do not worry about things like clothing or the language; the Cantonese cannot tell one white man from the other. All you have to do is playact. That is unless Herr Kenaghan wants to relive his war days and teach the Nationalists a thing or two."

Kenaghan shook his head.

"Very well, then. The fortunes of the Nationalists do not concern us. It is another fortune that we are after. The fortune, gentlemen, is in Sichuan."

"That's one hell of a hike, colonel."

"Indeed, it is."

"And we would have to go through a lot of Indian country to get there," Kenaghan said.

"Right again, but I can provide excellent cover. You see, several Nationalist divisions, including my own, are scheduled to begin operations in Sichuan soon. The party wants to subsume the province before the Ma clique gets there. It is a race against time, as the Ma armies have already left Xinjiang."

"Why should we care about fighting the Muslims?"

"Because I have it on good authority that Ma and his men stumbled upon some Russian gold in Kashgar. They plan on transporting it to Gansu, but first want to expand their power in the southwest. Hence, why they are planning on seizing Sichuan."

"What I don't get," Bergstrom said, "is why the Ma clique and the Nationalists would fight. I thought that they were allies."

"No such thing as allies in China, Herr Bergstrom. The only loyalty is to lucre. Besides, the Ma clique only care about securing power for their co-ethnics in the center. At this moment, Canton wants secularism and a unified state. The Ma armies stand in the way of that. They are headed for a showdown in Sichuan. That's why we will go there."

"And fight?" Kenaghan asked.

"Maybe, but our objective is the gold, Herr Kenaghan. We will get that gold, and I will take my cut back to Berlin. You too may do with the gold what you like."

"A standard 1/3 division for the job?" Bergstrom asked.

"Although I feel entitled to more because of the risks to my reputation involved," Colonel von Oppersdorff said, "I can agree to a simple three-way split."

"Excellent! Then it's settled," Bergstrom said.

"Almost. I only need you to confirm for me one thing: are you men willing to kill, and to possibly lose your immortal souls for the sake of gold?"

Bergstrom laughed and said that he would fight his own grandmother for gold.

"And what about you, Herr Kenaghan?"

"Just give me a reason to fight, and I'll show up."

Satisfied, Oppersdorff beckoned for a waiter and ordered schnapps for the entire table. The men drank and reminisced about the war until the sun came up and the Jade Dragon closed.

LIKE A LOT of ex-patriates living in the Orient, Inspector Clive Lewis felt like a man adrift. He was still quite young, and all the long-time Shanghailanders never let him forget his age. They, the well-heeled and moneyed financial managers and bureaucrats originally from London, saw Inspector Lewis as a novelty. The short, stocky policeman with the broad Yorkshire accent made them laugh, and not in a good-natured way. To the rich, Inspector Lewis was an uppity country bumpkin who had no business enforcing the law on *them*. Of course, they were all for him cracking Chinese skulls. That was his purpose, after all. In their eyes, Inspector Lewis and the Shanghai Municipal Police existed as a praetorian guard for the foreigners seeking all the benefits of the city with none of its darkness.

Inspector Lewis therefore found himself in a sticky situation when, on the night of the 13th, he was dispatched to the home of Hugh Morrison. Morrison's spacious mansion sat within spitting distance of the Bund and was well-known throughout the European community as the place to go for good alcohol and food.

· · ·

Morrison, despite specializing in the dreary business of machine parts, was a noted *bon vivant* beloved by all the right people in Shanghai. All the right people except for one, apparently.

Inspector Lewis stooped down and inspected the corpse of Hugh Morrison. "Looks like he had a terrible fright before death, don't you think?" Sergeant Grant agreed with the inspector's assessment.

"Makes sense to me that a man would look aghast as someone plunged that into him," Grant used his pencil to point at the Italian stiletto standing straight up in Morrison's chest.

"Quite right. Any word on suspects?"

"Not one."

"Who's in the house, then?"

Grant flipped upon a small notebook and began reading off a short list of names. "There's the housekeepers. A married couple from Wales. Both elderly. Claim that they slept through the whole thing. Another is the gardener. His name is Gomes or Gomes. I'm not too sure. He's a Portuguese from Macau and his English is not good. He claims that he goes home to his apartment every after-noon at five. We don't know yet when the murder occurred but seems like it happened late at night."

"Does this Portuguese fellow have access to the house?" Lewis asked.

"Yes. He has a big ring o' keys."

"We'll have to keep him as a suspect then."

"Right. Talked to the cook, too. He's another one that goes home, but he tends to stay much later seeing as Mr. Morrison likes...er liked...to entertain guests late into the night. He also has access to the home. The last on the list is the *amah*. She's Chinese like the cook. She stays here. Has a room in on the ground floor near the kitchen."

"A nanny? I did not know that Morrison had a child."

"Few did," Grant said. "The law says that Morrison is a bachelor. That is correct as Morrison never married the mother of his child. I got this information from everyone in the home, so I tend to accept it as true."

"An illicit dalliance, I see."

"More than that, sir. The mother herself is a chorus girl. A White Russian. Could be quite a scandal if the press finds out."

"It is up to us to make sure that they do not," Inspector Lewis added. If there was one thing that the Yorkshireman knew, it was that the Shanghailanders expected to keep their dirt secret, and they expected the Shanghai Municipal Police to do it for them. Lewis expelled a sigh of exhaustion. He dismissed Sergeant Grant with instructions to investigate the exterior of the home. As for him, Lewis got down to businesses looking for clues inside of the home.

The body of Hugh Morrison showed obvious signs of a struggle. The wealthy industrialist died with eyes as big as saucers, and a face partially blue and purple. Someone had tried to strangle him first, Lewis noted. He knew from experience that suffocating a man was hard work. Killing a man in general was harder than most expected. Inspector Lewis knew that from first-hand experience. He had seen death a lot in his life, from the hot furnaces of Sheffield to the battlefields of Flanders, but Shanghai topped them all. Nothing shocked him anymore after so many years spent patrolling the city and observing its filthy habits, from relentless opium consumption to the tradition of depositing unwanted babies into household drawers.

Lewis used his handkerchief to remove the stiletto. The stamping on its blade indicated that it was indeed Italian, made and manufactured in the city of Brescia. An Italian stiletto was a rare weapon in Shanghai, where most crimes were committed with common hatchets or butcher knives.

This information made Lewis think that the killer was a foreigner like Morrison, possibly an Italian. Lewis made a mental note to hunt down Morrison's address book and scour it for potential suspects.

The murder had occurred in Morrison's private study. It was a large, spacious room with a vaunted ceiling. Half of the room was covered by bookshelves made of dark mahogany. The other half was decorated with expensive trinkets like globes, bejeweled cuspidors, and several lacquered boxes. Morrison's body lay behind his glass-and-wooden desk.

"Attacked at his desk, no doubt," Lewis mumbled to himself. "Somebody he knew, I suspect." Lewis studied the contents of Morrison's desk. Everything seemed to be business related: invoices of shipments to and from Shanghai, a report from a factory in Liverpool, and a large ledger recording the costs and earnings from all of Morrison's investments in Europe and Asia. The fact that these items were left intact and in plain view showed that the murder was not motivated by money. Something else, possibly something personal drove someone to murder Hugh Morrison.

Lewis glanced at Morrison's impressive library. Again, most of the books were related to the world of business. It seemed that the deceased industrialist had no interests beyond making money and having nightly parties. A simple worldview but not a simple man, Lewis noted.

Without much thought, Lewis pulled from the bookshelf a book. Unlike its peers, the volume's title intrigued Lewis simply because it was so out-of-place. It proved to be a large history of the English Civil War. When Inspector Lewis reached and removed the large tome from its place, he heard a subtle click. He knew what the sound was—it was the familiar noise of a locked door being opened. Lewis hunted for the door.

He found it behind the bookshelf itself, as a section proved to contain a hidden compartment that swung inward. The knowledge stunned Lewis; he had read about secret passageways and hidden rooms in a million detective stories, but he always assumed that they were purely fictional. Here he found proof of their existence, and the knowledge intrigued him. Inspector Lewis entered the secret room.

The room behind the bookshelf was no bigger than a confessional. It was entirely dark, too. Lewis groped around for some light. His outstretched hand managed to find the shape of a candle. He used his matchbox to light it. The lit and lone black candle revealed a barren room composed only of single a cushion on the floor. The indents in the pillow were in the shape of a man's knees. The secret room served some kind of religious purpose. It even had an altar.

Except, judging by the pattern of dust on the wooden altar, a book was missing. For some reason, Lewis doubted that the missing volume was the Bible.

"Mr. Morrison is missing a book," Lewis said to the first member of the household that he could find. It proved to be one of the housekeepers, Mrs. Welles.

"A book?" she said with hesitancy. "I never knew Mr. Morrison to be much of a reader."

"His study says something else, and so too does the secret room."

"A secret room?" Inspector Lewis told her about his findings. The elderly woman swore up and down that she was unaware of such a room. Her husband said much the same. The rest of the house, from the surly gardener to the overly friendly *amah*, all agreed that they had never heard the deceased speak of a secret shrine. They all also said that, to their knowledge, Mr. Morrison and religion did not mix.

"All he cared about were parties," Mrs. Welles said. "I hate to speak ill of the dead, but I hated those parties. Lots of strange characters always coming and going."

"Strange how?" Lewis asked.

"The chorus girls were one thing," the elderly Welsh woman said, "but it was the menfolk who bothered me most of all. What a secretive lot! Never could get a straight answer out of them. All said they were in business, but none of them acted like Mr. Morrison."

"Please tell me more," Lewis said.

"What my wife means, sir, is that Mr. Morrison liked to entertain gentlemen. To our way of life, they were weird. Lots of them had beards and spoke with foreign accents. Some looked like rough customers. I come from the coal valleys, so I know hard men," Mr. Welles said.

"I think they're all anarchists, myself. Probably blackmailing Mr. Morrison," Mrs. Welles said.

"I don't know about that, Constance, but the American gentlemen is certainly involved in something obscene. Of that, I am sure."

"Who is this American fellow?" Lewis asked.

"All I know is Mr. Morrison introduced him as Marsh. Said he came from Massachusetts. Cannot remember the name of the town."

"Do you know where I can contact this man Marsh? Also, know where I can contact all the men who frequented this house?"

"Best to consult Mr. Morrison's address book. I can show you where it is if you follow me." Mr. Welles took Inspector Lewis back into the study.

· · ·

The old but hardy Welshmen made sure to avert his eyes from the corpse as he searched inside the desk for the address book. He found the object and handed it to Lewis. It was a simple brown leather address book, and, to Lewis's surprise, it was relatively blank.

"Thank you for your help, Mr. Welles."

"Anything for poor Mr. Morrison. Do you really think one of his friends did this?"

"We must consider all possibilities. I can assure you that we will solve this case and achieve justice for the late Mr. Morrison." Inspector Lewis typically avoided making such promises, but the warm eyes of the gray-haired butler reminded him of his late father.

The two men shook hands. Lewis found his way out of the house and into the streets. He and Sergeant Grant swapped information as they walked back to the stationhouse.

"Something religious then?" Grant asked.

"I'm not sure, but someone definitely took a book from that room. I don't know which or what kind of book, but what I saw in that room reminded me of a medieval monastery."

"Never can have a simple murder in Shanghai, can we?"

"I'm afraid not, Sergeant Grant."

After a half-hour walk, the two police officers reached the stationhouse. Grant stayed on the first floor to speak with the on-duty desk sergeant (a Chinese officer whose name Lewis never bothered to learn), while Lewis went up to the third floor. There he found the homicide bureau and his cluttered desk. After greeting the men on duty, and hearing a ribald joke from the irrepressible Scotsman, Inspector Robertson, Lewis sat down at his desk and began pouring through Morrison's address book. When he was done, Lewis had a full sheet of paper with names and addresses.

With list in hand, Lewis first cross-checked the names with Criminal Records. The Shanghai Municipal Police enjoyed quality intelligence, bountiful resources, and enough records on all the ex-pats of Asia to make them worried (that is, if they knew). The SMP's Special Branch was even superior to its British ancestor, although Lewis knew better than to ever say that out loud, especially anywhere outside of the confines of Foochow Road.

The first few names on the list generated nothing. The men seemed as clean as a whistle. This was not the case for one Aleksandr Sakolov. Lewis learned that he had a previous conviction in London for armed robbery as well as a similar charge in Riga. A note from the Special Branch told Lewis that Sakolov may or may not have converted to Bolshevism while serving in the Russian military during the Great War. A certain Inspector Lippincott wrote in bold pen, "SUSPECTED COMITERN AGENT. IS UNDER SURVEILLANCE." The presence of Aleksandr Sakolov in Hugh Morrison's address book lent credence to Mrs. Welles's theory of radical intrigue.

Another questionable customer was the American Jeremiah Marsh. The file recorded Marsh's hometown as a certain Innsmouth in Massachusetts. The Essex County Sheriff's Department had arrested Marsh on several counts of bootlegging and smuggling. A true descendant of his Yankee forebearers, Marsh apparently took to the sea aboard a tramp steamer after his last conviction. He then promptly abandoned ship for Shanghai. How he came to haunt the Morrison residence and why was unknown.

The last two names on Lewis's list troubled him the most, even though by all accounts the men were respectable representatives of their class. The first was a Captain Umberto Lucchini. Lucchini was one of the officers of Rome's military mission to the Nationalist government in Canton.

. . .

A decorated ace of Italy's conquest of Libya and its war against the Austrians, Captain Lucchini was supposedly headquartered in the south, and yet he found time to frequent Morrison's home in Shanghai. Lewis wondered to himself about whether Captain Lucchini knew anything about his country's famous stilettos.

Lewis found another military man on the list—Colonel Friedrich von Oppersdorff. Like Lucchini, Oppersdorff was attached to the Nationalist forces in Canton. His job, Lewis learned, was turn to Nationalist soldiers into Asia's Prussians. Colonel Oppersdorff would know, as his file showed that he came from a *junker* family native to East Prussia. Two high-ranking military advisors frequenting the home of a British magnate was not surprising, as foreigners congregated among themselves in the International Settlement. No, what worried Lewis was the presence of these men in Shanghai, a city threatened by Nationalist expansion. The Municipal Council's policy was eager to keep the Nationalists out of the city and far away from the wealth of the foreigners. Men like Lucchini and Oppersdorff's threatened Shanghai's status as a free city-state in the heart of China, and it was possible that they had an accomplice in Hugh Morrison. Worst still, all three hob-knobbed with the common criminal Marsh and the suspected Bolshevik agent Sakolov. What bound these men together? It was Lewis's duty to find out.

With plenty of sun left in an unusually bright day, Lewis hit the streets again. His plan was to pay a visit to Jeremiah Marsh. He figured that Sakolov already had an SMP tail, plus the wily Russian would likely be on high alert if he ever crossed paths with a stranger. Lewis knew from many years of surveillance that the bad guys needed to see their police shadows often, but more experienced villains had a preternatural ability to spot a policeman.

· · ·

Lewis decided based on this information, and he similarly believed that Marsh would be the more compliant of the two. A low-level smuggler would be easier to manage, Inspector Lewis reasoned.

Jeremiah Marsh lived in the French Concession right by the Yangjingnbang stream that followed into Huangpu River. The location confused Lewis, as it was a better-than-average road in one of the cleaner parts of the settlement. Despite his background and reputation, Marsh was living well in China. Or so it seemed at first. Lewis learned after entering the address listed in Marsh's Special Branch file that the American worked as a janitor at the location. He lived on the premises in a basement room. The porter who showed Lewis to it warned him that Marsh was most likely asleep, as he worked nights. Lewis knew he had to tread carefully, as the SMP did not enjoy full jurisdiction in the French concession. It was official policy to contact the gendarmes first, but Lewis plowed ahead alone.

"That is great news. We police thrive on surprise," Lewis said after winking at the slightly stunned porter. When the other man left, Lewis pounded hard on the door. He received no answer.

"Jeremiah Marsh? Open up. It's the police."

Still nothing. Lewis struck the door several more times and repeated himself. This time there was a response of sorts. Lewis pressed his ear to the door and heard the tell-tale noise of running feet. Lewis unholstered his Colt 1908 and kicked the door at its hinges. The wood proved stout, so Lewis simply shot the doorknob to gain entry. While reaching through the bullet-made hole, a second shot, this one fired from inside of the room, rung out. Miraculously the shot missed wide, leaving the shocked Lewis unscratched.

Lewis pulled the door open and fired into the dark room. Another shot responded, and again it missed wide.

"Stop firing, Marsh!"

"Go to hell," a voice bellowed from the darkness.

Marsh's decision to answer gave Lewis a chance to find his range. The policeman narrowed his dominant eye to focus, trained his automatic on one corner in the room, and let off two shots in succession. He then took cover and waited for a return volley. When none came, he entered the room.

Marsh's living quarters were as disheveled as he proved to be. Lewis tripped over papers, empty whisky bottles, and stacks of pulp magazines. The same items were found scattered on the cover-less mattress and underneath its wire frame. Lewis wondered how the man ever managed to sleep.

He found Marsh crumbled up near a corner dresser. One of Lewis's bullets had entered the man's chest right beneath the collarbone. It was a fatal blow. A quick check of Marsh's pulse confirmed that the American was dead. Lewis groaned when he realized that he would have to return to the station to complete the necessary paperwork. After shoeing away curious onlookers from the building (most of whom were the sleepy-looking employees of the night shift), Lewis got down to inspecting the room. It was the second death scene he had looked at that day.

Unlike the Morrison mansion, Marsh's quarters were miniscule. The bed and chest were it; everything else was clutter. The papers on Marsh's floor were unimportant odds and ends—receipts, images torn from magazines and newspapers, and more than a few "Paris pictorials" that sailors loved to carry with them on long voyages. A sinking feeling came over Lewis. Yes, he had killed in self-defense, and was justified. And yet he still felt rotten for killing a man who owned so little.

Just before ending his search, Lewis explored the standalone dresser. The top drawer contained only a second change of clothes. Marsh's frugal attire matched his living arrangements, as the collar, shirt, and pants were both threadbare and dirty. His socks had holes in them as well. In life, Marsh cared little about comfort or amenities. Yet, in the bottom drawer, Lewis discovered something that Marsh clearly cared about.

It was a book wrapped in a clean piece of cloth. Lewis opened it and found an old volume bound in black leather. The outside was bare and contained no information. The frontispiece, written in both red and black ink, claimed that the book was *Unaussprechlichen Kulten* by a certain Friedrich von Junzt. Lewis cracked the spine and saw indecipherable pages in Latin and German. He remembered the missing book from Morrison's hidden shrine and wondered aloud if Herr von Junzt's work was the book in question. Lewis tucked the volume underneath his arm and exited the room. His next stop was the building's lone telephone, which he used to contact the desk sergeant on duty. Lewis waited until uniformed officers arrived, and then walked into the night.

"What is this?" Johansen asked after Lewis slammed the book on his desk. Lewis knew that the workaholic Johansen would still be attending to his business well after five o'clock. He was right, of course. The Norwegian officer of the Scandinavian Company was one of the only men left in the barracks.

"It is a book that I would like you to translate."

"In a city crawling with academics, you came to me, a humble soldier, with a request to translate what appears to be a very long book."

"You are the only friend I know who speaks German, plus you are one of the few men who I trust in this metropolis."

"Where did you find this book?"

"Between you and me, it is evidence. I found it at a crime scene."

"Aren't there guidelines about handling such things? You bringing this book to me feels like a violation somehow," Johansen said.

"It is, but what's a broken rule between friends?"

Johansen was one of the few full-time staff officers of the Shanghai Volunteer Corps, the foreign colony's auxiliary militia. Officially, Johansen was Lewis's superior, as the SMP inspector was only a sergeant in the British "A" Company, and a reservist at that. And yet the two men had an easy friendship born of their shared backgrounds. The Yorkshireman saw a lot of himself in the soul and spirit of the fisherman's son from Bergen.

"Did this book have anything to do with your crime?" Johansen asked.

"Possibly. I've investigated two deaths today. The first one was a murder where I noted that a book was missing. The second death, which I caused, included that book on the premises."

"Did you just admit to murder?"

"Pure self-defense, chap. The villain shot first." Johansen raised an eyebrow at Lewis, which caused the policemen to smile.

"If you are suspicious, then call the police," he said.

"I see. *Unaussprechlichen Kulten* by Friedrich von Junzt. Printed in Dusseldorf in 1839. Rare book, I presume."

"What does the title mean?"

"It means 'Unspeakable Cults,' or something like 'Of Unspeakable Cults.' It is in the dative case, or my German is rustier than I remembered."

"A work of the occult?"

"So the title would suggest. Does your case deal with the dark arts?"

"I don't know yet."

"I'll tell you what," the Norwegian said, "I will give this a glance over tonight and tell you what I find in the morning. You can either stop by here or I will make a visit to your place of work this time."

"It is a deal, sir." Lewis made a mocking salute to his superior. Johansen returned it.

"Now leave me in peace. I need to finish something for the review board. I am trying to make captain.

"Best of luck. Being a captain is quite an achievement, even if you're nothing more than the leader of a handful of Swedes well past their fighting years. With that, Lewis left the barracks and made his way on foot to his apartment.

Lewis lived along the Nanking Road. He made a decent living as an inspector, plus he was pathologically averse to spending money. As a result, he managed to find a full-time apartment in one of the International Zone's better hotels. The mostly Chinese staff greeted him as he arrived. Lewis was polite, but curt. He tipped the bellboy a single British pound after he reached the fifth floor. His plan that evening was simple—write down his findings on the Morrison and Marsh cases, knock back a few glasses of whisky, and then sleep like a log. For him, sleeping was a rare pleasure. It also doubled as his pastime. At ten o'clock, after several hours of writing and drinking, Lewis turned off his lights and climbed into bed. He was asleep within ten minutes.

At three o'clock, while Inspector Lewis slept soundly, a black-clad figure climbed its way up the face of the hotel. With unnatural speed and dexterity, along with movements more akin to a spider's than a man's, the figure climbed over the rough stonework until it reached the fifth floor.

. . .

After moving northwards, the figure began moving west to east until it reached a single window. A brief paused followed before the figure disappeared completely only to re-emerge, mist-like, inside of the sleeping detective's room.

The figure began searching. It slowly opened drawers and rooted around in Lewis's closet. The figure even dared to stand next to the sleeping policeman and inspect his body. Whatever it was, the object of the figure's search was not found. Just as quietly as the figure had arrived, it escaped out into the night and climbed down the hotel like Count Dracula descending his castle.

It was all over by 3:03 a.m.

CHAPTER 3

THE BEST PLANS OF MICE AND MEN

BERGSTROM COMPLAINED the whole train ride down to Canton. He complained about the lackluster food service, the lack of quality spirits, and the hardness of the seats.

"And top it all off, we have these horrific uniforms to wear," he said while pulling at the hem of his tunic.

Kenaghan growled to show his annoyance. But, in truth, he felt the same way as his partner. His bigger concern was the South China heat, which came in thick and heavy through the train's windows. The upper portions of his own tunic were ringed with sweat.

"Khaki really isn't your color," Bergstrom said as a joke to his perspiring partner.

"It may not be my color, but I've worn it before," Kenaghan said.

"I tell you what, all this misery better be worth it. It what our German friend says is true, then we could be sitting pretty for the rest of our lives."

"Not with the way you spend money, Swede."

• • •

"Don't be angry that I enjoy the finer things in life, Yank." The two continued to rib each other until the train stopped in the city. It was their way of taking their minds off the discomfort. However, all the kidding in the world could not stop them from being miserable in Canton. The oppressive humidity and the putrid smells assailed them, even in the more modern confines of the British-built train station. A tactless Bergstrom placed his scented handkerchief to his nose and kept it there until Oppersdorff's chauffer arrived to escort them to a waiting green-and-black Packard. Bergstrom did not drop his self-made mask until the car stopped at the barracks.

Oppersdorff greeted the men at the gates of the brand-new Whampoa Military Academy. The oppressive weather seemed to bother the Prussian little, as he stood stick-necked and pristine in his field gray army uniform.

"Welcome to the future of China," Oppersdorff said with a wry smile.

"The future stinks. Quite literally," Bergstrom said.

"One gets used to it. Still, I share you opinion of this land. A dirty and heathen country."

"That is a fine way to speak of your charges," Kenaghan said.

"You will soon see for yourself the quality of the Chinese recruit." With that the trio passed the guards at the gate and entered the grounds. The place was a mixture of white marble and gray stone. It looked clean, but spare. As they passed the barracks rooms, which were made of lacquered wood and paper below roofs of rounded tiles, Oppersdorff let his true opinions be known.

"The lads who sleep in those rooms could not shine the shoes of a French peasant, let alone a Pomeranian grenadier. Most are illiterate serfs. Even the officer corps show limited intelligence. The only ones who are worthy of a modicum of respect are the men from Shandong and the veterans. The soldiers from Shandong are bigger and stronger than the rest, plus they like me because they all have fond memories of Kiautschou."

Oppersdorff blew out a thick ring of cigarette smoke before continuing with his diatribe. "As for the veterans, many of them fled the warlords of the north. One would assume that they preferred the Three Principles of the People to the venality of the warlords. One would be incorrect, however. They were bandits before serving, and they are still bandits now. They are just more disciplined and skilled bandits. Then of course there are the communists, or rather the secret communists. We have not been able to prove anything, but there exists the possibility that some of my men are Bolshevik agents or loyal to the local communist rabble that calls itself a party."

"And yet you think this motley crew can defeat the Muslims in Sichuan?" Kenaghan asked.

"I do not care one way or the other. The Muslims have a fierce reputation as fighters, and I do not doubt that the rumors are true. If my Nationalists get slaughtered, I will not shed a tear. All I care about is getting that gold and never seeing China again."

"Now, as for you two," Oppersdorff said, "you must pretend to be fellow trainers for the next few weeks while I finalize the plan. Do not worry about the accuracy of your drills, just pantomime to the best of your ability. You will only be dealing with small companies."

"Aren't we expected to be German? I can't speak the language," Kenaghan said.

"It tickles me that you think these peasants know the difference between German and Arabic. All foreign tongues sound the same to them, so feel free to bark in English or Swedish if you want."

"Barking is for dogs, Herr Colonel, but if you insist, I will." Bergstrom laughed and slapped Kenaghan on the back. "Now, let's talk about lunch."

"Follow me to my private quarters."

For over an hour the three men shared a bottle of schnapps and glasses of brandy. They dined on pork spareribs cooked in the style of Northern China, plus Oppersdorff regaled them with delicacies like bread, sausages, and cheese. He told Kenaghan and Bergstrom that the items had come courtesy of the black market.

"One can have almost anything in the south for just pfennigs. Even flesh is available."

"Sounds fantastic to me! To flesh, gentlemen!" Bergstrom raised a toast. Before the others could join, there was a knock on Oppersdorff's door. The Prussian stood and answered it. On the other side was a short and thin man with a large and very black mustache.

"Come on in! There is plenty of food."

The little man bowed at the waist and pulled up a seat at the table. He had already picked out morsels of food by the time Oppersdorff bothered to make introductions.

"This is Captain Lucchini. He is here to teach our peasants how to fly." Bergstrom and Kenaghan both greeted the captain.

"And these men are here to help us rob the Muslims blind!" Kenaghan was taken aback by admission. Shock and surprise washed over his usually serene countenance.

"Do not be alarmed, Herr Kenaghan. Captain Lucchini has my utmost confidence. We were partners in this endeavor before I contacted Herr Bergstrom in Shanghai."

"Never to worry," Lucchini said in pidgin English, "we get the gold together."

"I accept your assurances. I just am a little suspicious whenever conspiracies grow unexpectedly," Kenaghan said.

"Your hesitancy is a strength. It is good to be always on-guard. The Orient is a brimming with treachery, but not from us. We are all Europeans after all," Oppersdorff leaned back and emitted large smoke rings. Lucchini followed suit.

"Do you have a plan yet? I mean, do you know how we are going to pull off this heist?" Bergstrom asked.

"We have a plan, yes," Lucchini said. Oppersdorff got up from his seat, opened a roll-top desk, and pulled from within a rolled pieced of paper. He cleared a few dishes and unfurled the item. Kenaghan and Bergstrom craned their necks to see a map of Sichuan penned in Chinese characters but riddled with notes in Italian and German.

"The current plan is to attack the Ma force through this pass here and here. Our general thinks that he can bottle up the Muslims, and that's why he plans on sending a diversion force through the valley first to draw Ma's attention. A feigned retreat is the oldest tactic of the Mongols, and the people here have never forgotten its effectiveness."

"We will be that diversion force," Lucchini echoed. "We go into the valley."

"Yes, we will spearhead the surprise attack, but we will not retreat. I will not listen to my commander's orders. I will also not attack where he wants me too. Instead, we will attack the rear, for that is where the baggage train will be. And where the baggage train is, the gold will be there too. My plan is to smash the rear, grab the gold, and then flee into the hills. From there we will set out for Chengdu. I have already chartered a private plane at an aerodrome. All we have to do is make sure we arrive safe and sound."

Bergstrom smiled and slapped his hands together in joy. Kenaghan was more subdued in his response.

What followed were several days of drudgery, or at least drudgery for Kenaghan. Unlike Bergstrom, who mostly stayed in his quarters smoking and drinking, Kenaghan took training seriously. He knew what it was like to the be thrown into combat unprepared, and although he had no special feelings for the recruits, he still recoiled at the thought of them being slaughtered like sitting ducks. So, through curses and kicks, Kenaghan spent two weeks trying to turn the men into real soldiers. He saw some improvement in their rifle shooting, but not much else.

At the end of the fortnight, Kenaghan figured that he had worked hard for nothing, and that maybe Bergstrom had the right view of things. Bergstrom certainly thought so, and he took an interest in twisting the knife in Kenaghan's conscience.

"You looked like a real drill sergeant out there. Too bad that you should have been getting drunk instead," the Swede would say to his American counterpart. Kenaghan would always growl as a response. The banter between the two men tickled Lucchini, while the stoic Prussian never so much as batted an eye. To Kenaghan, Oppersdorff seemed focused but also full of secrets. He had experienced men like him before—serious, stern, and evasive. It was not a good combination.

"I am somewhat weary of our Prussian friend," Kenaghan confided in Bergstrom on the night before their departure to the wilds of Sichuan.

"How so?" Kenaghan laid out all his suspicions and inchoate feelings. Bergstrom nodded along, but Kenaghan could tell that he was not listening. When Kenaghan finished, Bergstrom leaned back and cradled the back of his head in his hands.

"The problem with you is that you worry too much. See, look at me. Do I worry? No! All my mind is concerned with right now is the money. That's what you should focus on too. Your life would improve if you did."

"Maybe," was all the reply that Kenaghan could muster.

Hours later, not long after dawn, the two men found themselves standing on the parade ground inspecting the troops under their supervision. While Oppersdorff conducted some last-minute drills, Kenaghan took stock of the equipment. There was little uniformity in materiel. Oppersdorff carried a 1908 Luger. Bergstrom and Kenaghan had each been given FN Model 1900 pistols that had been manufactured in China at the Linjing Arsenal. Bergstrom kept his, while Kenaghan had traded his for a Webley revolver.

Lucchini sported an absurdly large Colt Model 1900 that he had to carry in a leg holster that covered most of his slender thigh. As for the men, Kenaghan cringed seeing that most had been issued C96 "broomhandle" pistols as their primary arms. The 7.63x25mm round was not known for its stopping power, and Kenaghan knew that they would be less than useless in the higher altitudes of Sichuan. The only hope, he thought, would be if the Muslims were similarly armed. A few lucky soldiers had Hanyang 88 rifles (a Chinese version of the German Gewehr 88), while the even more lucky carried Russian-made Mosin-Nagant rifles. The entire force only contained two machine guns, both being heavy 1910 Maxims that required whole squads to transport.

At noon, the men and their officers were loaded into trains bound for the Sichuan border. The soldiers sat in the far rear, while the foreign officers enjoyed the first-class carriage. Oppersdorff, shrouded in cigarette smoke, informed Bergstrom and Kenaghan that the train journey would be a long one, as the poor quality of the rails of the interior, along with the necessity of bribing Hunan, Guangai, and Guzhou warlords, was bound to slow them down.

"So, by all means, get as comfortable as possible," Oppersdorff said.

For the first two nights, then men played cards, smoked, and drank. They swapped stories. Bergstrom started first, and Oppersdorff and Lucchini seemed to enjoy the Swedish scamp's many tales of misadventure and sexual conquest. Lucchini especially liked Bergstrom's reminiscences about the buxom blondes of his native Stockholm. He joined in the theme by talking about his girlfriends in Milan and Turin, as well as the many prostitutes he frequented while on the Isonzo front. Oppersdorff, on the other hand, spoke only of war. His tales were full of blood and guts, trench mud, and rifle fire. He compared life on the Eastern Front to the one in France.

Of the two, Oppersdorff much preferred the more mobile fighting in the Carpathians. He even had good things to say about his former Austrian allies, although he added that they only fought well under German command. Oppersdorff talked well into the night. He only paused when he noticed that Bergstrom and Lucchini were both fast asleep.

"It is now your turn to speak of your experiences, Herr Kenaghan."

"I would rather not. My war was not as adventurous as yours."

"I highly doubt that," Oppersdorff said. "But let us talk about something other than war. Would you like a ghost story before bed?"

"A ghost story? We are not children."

"Ghost stories for children are all about imparting wisdom and morals. The story I am about to tell is true, or at least the people of

Sichuan believe it to be true." Oppersdorff struck up a new cigarette. He offered a fresh one from his case to Kenaghan. The American accepted.

"The story concerns a ridge of haunted mountains. Not too different from the Harz Mountains in my country. The locals call the mountains *Heiren xiongdi hui*. That roughly translates to the "black brotherhood." The mountains are said to be abnormally black, with dark trees on each slope. The villages in the area stay as far away from the mountains as possible."

"Is it tigers?" Kenaghan inquired.

"There could be tigers, like there could be bears. But that is not what they are afraid of. They're afraid of *Mi-Gul Shan*. The origin of this word is uncertain, and it does not directly translate to anything. Scholars of Mandarin linguistics consider it jumbled nonsense. A small minority argue that it's a word of proto-Old Chinese origin whose meaning has been lost to time. Either way, the Mi-Gul Shan are dreaded."

"What are they?" Kenaghan asked.

"That is not easily answered. They could be spirits of the mountain, ghosts of tortured souls, or demonic entities from the earth prison, which the Chinese call *Diyu*. That is their version of hell, in case you did not know. But there is one story that claims that the Mi-Gul Shan are gods, or rather were gods long before humans populated this planet. Few artistic renderings of them exist, but there is one that I saw in Peking years ago. The Beiyang government keep it locked away and out of the view of the public now for reasons of national pride. You see, the artist was a psychotic hermit who was arrested by the dying Qing government for 'disturbing the peace.' I can confirm that the statuette of a Mi-Gul Shan that he crafted and that I saw was disturbing. It looked like a giant salamander, except the statuette depicted the creature as standing on two legs. It also lacked a mouth, which interested me as the sculptor supposedly claimed at his trial that his muse spoke to him."

"How did this hermit discover the creature in the first place?"

"The hermit lived in a village that existed in the shadow of the Black Brotherhood. He made a sparse living collecting wild mushrooms. Because of his closeness to the cursed mountains, his neighbors shunned him. As a result, he increasingly spent more and more time on the mountains, even going so far as to sleep there during the summer.

"It was during one of those summer nights that he spied the temple. He described the structure as ghostly white in the wan moonlight, with a pointed black roof and black columns that gleamed even the darkness. The funny thing is that no structure has ever been recorded on the Black Brotherhood, for they have been considered cursed since time immemorial. And yet the hermit not only saw the temple but visited it too."

"He entered the temple?" Kenaghan asked with shock and surprise in his voice.

"Yes. The man was insane, and that insanity made him fearless. He entered the temple and found many torches burning, as if there were still priests there. Except there was no one—the temple was empty like a tomb. In the center, at the heart of the structure, the hermit claimed he found a large statue of a Mi-Gul Shan. This statue was made of a strange stone that combined obsidian and jade. The hermit approached the statue and reached out to touch it. It was then that a voice spoke to him. The voice told him not to touch the structure, but to study it with his eyes. The voice told him to memorize the statue and a make a version for himself.

When the hermit searched for the source of the voice, he discovered an elongated shadow in the firelight. The shadow extended from the rear of the statue. When the shadow moved and moved closer to the firelight, the hermit ran screaming back out into the mountains.

"The next morning, the hermit searched in vain for the temple. He could neither find it or any evidence of its existence. He went back to his village and told everyone he found about the temple. Most ignored him, while the headman struck him and officially banished him. Unsure of what to do, the hermit dedicated himself to creating and completing the statuette. He finished it after several weeks. He began showing the figure to the travelers he encountered. Word soon spread of a crazy man of the mountains showing off an ugly and unclean statuette to unsuspecting individuals. The accounts eventually reached the governor-general in charge of Sichuan. He ordered the hermit arrested and put on trial. The rest, they say, is history. The statuette was confiscated by the government and transported far away to a museum in Peking. As for the hermit, his head was severed by a military executioner."

"That is one of the wildest stories I have ever heard," Kenaghan said.

"Indeed. It is true, or at least mostly true. The court records exist, and so too does the statuette."

"Yes, but do you believe in the existence of the Mi-Gul Shan?"

Oppersdorff leaned back and thought a little. "Whether or not I believe in them is immaterial. The locals certainly do, and most of our soldiers do as well. The superstitions around the Mi-Gul Shan are a benefit to us, too."

"How so?"

A sharp, carnivorous smile flashed on Oppersdorff's lips. "The pig-headed General Ma is moving his troops right through the Black Brotherhood. As a Muslim, he refuses to believe in pagan superstitions. He is thus forcing his men to move through a haunted country in order to circumvent the routes most commonly used by Chinese armies. I'll wager most of what I own that his men will be paralyzed with fear, and our appearance will be considered a manifestation of the Mi-Gul Shan."

"And thus, easy pickings," Kenaghan added.

"Even easier than hunting lame stags," Oppersdorff said.

The train journey continued for days afterwards. Kenaghan studied the landscape as it transitioned from flat plains to mountains. The tall and rounded peaks of the mountains reminded Kenaghan of the ancient Appalachians back in Pennsylvania. Whenever he pulled the windows down, strong smells of spice, especially the locally grown peppercorn flooded the train compartment. Kenaghan loved the smell; his companions deplored it.

When the journey finally ended, the languor ceased, and a flurry of activity replaced it. Oppersdorff wasted no time in screaming at the soldiers to form their companies. The men departed the train with some organization, and before long were assembled by the train tracks into well-ordered rows. Oppersdorff told them in German to make their camp and get as much sleep as possible ahead of that night's raid. This was translated into Chinese by the various non-commissioned officers, who, despite their best efforts, only managed to get the men to pitch a few perfunctory tents. Most of the soldiers slept outside, using their kit bundles for pillows.

Rather than sleep, the four-man conspiracy studied and re-studied Oppersdorff's plan. They all memorized it, from their roles to the roles of the other men. In short, Oppersdorff, Lucchini, Bergstrom, and Kenaghan would break off and separate early in the attack. Kenaghan and Bergstrom were to carry out as much diversionary fire as possible so as to disorient Ma's men. As for Lucchini and Oppersdorff, one would seize the gold, while the other acted as security. All had permission to kill as many soldiers as possible. With that, all men ceased their discussions. They kept mum for the rest of the day, as the soldiers slept soundly around them.

The arrival of nighttime started the activity all over again. Orders were shouted, including the ironic order to keep all subsequent conversation to a whisper. The men were informed that they had a miles-long march in front of them. All were told to load their weapons and make them ready. After final checks, the small army began marching into the Sichuan wilderness.

"You will have noticed something," Oppersdorff whispered to Kenaghan, "nobody made mention of the Black Brotherhood."

"I will have to take your word for that," Kenaghan said.

"It is wise to keep these peasants in the dark about where we are going. We want the enemy to panic, not our own men."

"Do you really believe that that hoodoo tale has that much power over these people?"

"Absolutely. Of that I have no doubt."

The march was a struggle, as each step went up into higher altitudes. Kenaghan could hear the soldiers struggle to maintain steady breathing. Most of them came from the southern coast, where mountains were rare. This did not bode well for the attack, as Kenaghan knew that many of the men would be too exhausted to fight properly. He looked occasionally at Oppersdorff. The Prussian seemed unfazed by everything. Lucchini, on the other hand, seemed to being having fun, and the Italian practically skipped at times. Bergstrom joined in and always had a song or a whistle on his lips. Only Kenaghan remained morose.

"Never seen you smile, Herr Kenaghan," Oppersdorff whispered to him.

"We are marching towards death. What is there to smile about?"

"In battle there is joy. It is the only joy worth experiencing. I have felt that way since 1914. Don't you?" Kenaghan grunted.

"You remind me of antediluvian man, Kenaghan. All brutish barbarism and barely contained violence. I for one cannot wait to see you in action. It will be glorious!"

"I might disappoint you."

"Never. But maybe I should follow your lead and return to silence. We are nearing the climax. Notice the smoke rising below us."

Kenaghan smelled, rather than saw the smoke. Oppersdorff's words indicated that the fires were attached to the Muslim camp. Kenaghan had no reason to doubt it. Using his hands as eyes, he made sure that his revolver was loaded. Oppersdorff did the same. Once satisfied, the Prussian turned around and performed a series of hand signals that were passed down the line.

The men came to a sudden stop. They then formed into flying columns of squads within larger companies. The movements were well-executed. Oppersdorff motioned for them to hold their positions. The Prussian called the other officers to follow him, and Bergstrom, Lucchini, and Kenaghan followed behind as Oppersdorff found the edge of a small cliff.

The four men looked down and saw several campfires. Around each fire were several men dressed in the familiar blue-gray uniforms worn by their own men. From their vantage point, the Muslim army looked larger than their own force, and yet the lack of perimeter security was a clear sign that they did not expect enemy action. They heard the soldiers laugh and eat as if all was well in the world. They likely believed that they had already earned Sichuan all for themselves.

. . .

"Let's put our best riflemen up here. Also, place the machine guns here. They should have no problem slaughtering the Muslims to a man. This may be even easier than I thought," Oppersdorff said. Lucchini moved back towards the ranks to the spread the orders.

"That's what we are aiming for," Oppersdorff said, pointing to the rear of the camp. There, Kenaghan could see courtesy of limited firelight a large tent that was guarded by two soldiers with rifles. "That is where General Ma sleeps. A man like that would keep the gold as close as possible to his person." Oppersdorff grinned and slapped Kenaghan on the back.

"It is time for you to show me your calling, Herr Kenaghan." Lucchini returned with several men, including the machine gun companies. The two Maxims were silently settled along the cliff, with one aiming to the west and the other the east. In between were placed prone riflemen. Kenaghan looked over his shoulder and saw that the men had inched closer and either sat on their hunches or were fully prone in the dirt. Oppersdorff focused on his watch. He watched its hands tick by until, with a single hand on the shoulder of the nearest machine gunner, he gave the signal for the fusillade.

The night roared with invisible death, as bullets flew down into the valley with a tremendous velocity. The two Maxim gunners maintained steady tattoos of death, as they gently swung their barrels back and forth like the reaper's scythe. The riflemen beside them took longer to fire, but their Hanyang and Mosin rounds were more accurate. The bullets cut through cartilage and bones. Intestines were exposed, and at least one head was severed from its neck by a bullet. The machine guns and rifles provided covering fire too, as the mass of the soldiers flew down the side of the cliff and into the jaws of the enemy. Kenaghan saw more than a few men stumble and fall. He knew that their fates were at best horrific injuries, and at worse fatal breaks.

· · ·

More surprising was the ferocity of the soldiers. The trainees who had performed so poorly in drills back in Canton showed a sharp bloodlust when face-to-face against the Muslims. Kenaghan saw one Cantonese peasant bayonet a Muslim before shoving his wounded body into an open flame. Another unloaded his Mauser into multiple torsos before succumbing to a killing blow from an unseen rifle. The men proved their mettle as soldiers, and Kenaghan felt pride at the realization.

"Now is our time," Oppersdorff shouted. The two guards at the tent had left to join the battle, and Kenaghan could see a partially dressed General Ma shouting instructions while occasionally firing his Luger. Kenaghan followed Oppersdorff, who was the first man down the cliff. Lucchini was behind him, and Bergstrom was the last in line. The men reached the valley and formed a curved line. Oppersdorff, at the head, fired 9mm rounds at any man who approached him. Kenaghan likewise let rip with his .455 Webley, falling two beefy Muslim shoulders who charged him with bayonets. Even in the melee, Kenaghan could hear Lucchini singing as he took pot shots with his pistol. As for Bergstrom, he confined his shooting to the dead and wounded. Kenaghan grabbed the Swede by his collar as he stood over a squirming Muslim begging for his life.

"We don't do that type of thing," Kenaghan growled. The Swede was pulled back into the fray. Bullets whizzed everywhere, forcing the four conspirators to duck, and run towards the tent. Oppersdorff maintained point. Kenaghan marveled at the efficiency of the man. Oppersdorff was a Prussian killing machine who emptied and reloaded his pistol seconds after killing men standing to his front and flanks.

"With men like you, how did Germany ever lose the war?" Kenaghan shooting after firing his own shots.

"I'm not a man, but the avatar of Tyr. You are only getting a taste of my powers," Oppersdorff said. The gleam of a firelight in his eyes made him look possessed. Truly, the Prussian did fight like a god of war.

At last, they reached General Ma's tent. The corpulent general raised his Luger to stop their progress, but Oppersdorff proved quicker. His Luger recoiled once, and General Ma fell to the dirt. It was an unceremonious end for the old warrior, but the conspirators had no time for obituaries. They raced into the tent and began ransacking it. They turned over desks, tables, and chairs. Bergstrom even tore up the deceased general's bed. The gold was finally located in a footlocker. Oppersdorff broke the lock by shooting it twice. His greedy hands rushed to open the box. Inside, all four men saw five rows of stacked gold. Lucchini picked up the first bar and showed it to the others. He indicated that the seal on the bar proved that it was authentic Tsarist gold.

"Shall we divide it up now, or wait until we are in safer environs?" Bergstrom asked. The sounds of the fighting raging all around them. All agreed to a man to divide the spoils later. Kenaghan and Bergstrom picked up the footlocker and hefted it onto their shoulders while Oppersdorff and Lucchini provided front and rear security. The sounds of gunfire continued as the foursome made their escape. They could only walk quickly due to the weight of their haul.

They were forced to stop when several rifle rounds landed at Oppersdorff's feet. The bullets were followed by the bark of several Cantonese voices. The voices belonged to their own soldiers, who began surrounded them with their rifles and pistols at the ready.

"Put gold down now!" one soldier said in accented English.

"What are you doing?" Oppersdorff responded in kind.

"We are taking the gold. Put it down now."

"Like hell you are," Bergstrom shouted definitely in Swedish. A soldier moved in from the darkness and struck Bergstrom in the back of the neck with his rifle butt.

Lucchini raised his pistol to fire, but his arm was slashed with a bayonet. The blood spurted like the eruption of Mount Vesuvius. Another soldier picked Lucchini's fallen sidearm from the dirt and tucked into his belt.

"Stop fighting back and give us the gold!" The mutineer yelled.

"Let me guess," Oppersdorff said, "your paymasters work for the Comintern."

"Revolution is coming, you running dog. Money is for the revolution of all Chinese people!"

"Red," Kenaghan grumbled. An unseen mutineer gave him a quick kick in the pants. He turned around and punched the first face that he saw. Several rifle butts rained down on his head and shoulders. The footlocker fell from Kenaghan's shoulders and onto the dirt. Several soldiers rushed to picked it back up after shoving Bergstrom out of the way. The mutineers were in full control of the gold mere minutes after the four conspirators had stolen it themselves.

"Give us your weapons now!" The English-speaking soldier shouted. Bergstrom, Kenaghan, and Oppersdorff withstood several blows that were designed to encourage them to hand over their pistols and cartridges. Oppersdorff and Bergstrom handed their weapons and ammunition over. Kenaghan did too but only after using his elbow to strike one mutineer in the private parts. Several hands seized all for men and used knives to hack off their officer insignias. The bleeding Lucchini was kicked in the face by a dirty boot for no reason at all.

"Get up! On your feet, dogs!" The men were led away from the camp. They shuffled past dozens of dead bodies, Muslim and Cantonese alike. They marched beyond the camp and into the dark mountain wilderness. They were in total darkness when the mutineers halted.

"Now you have to survive. Goodnight, dogs." At that signal, the mutineers feel to bludgeoning the four foreigners with their hands and feet. They did not stop until all four were unconscious. Satisfied, the English-speaking man called out instructions in Cantonese. Eventually, the prone and unconscious men were all alone.

The mutineers had left them to a fate worse than death; they left the foreigners to face the Mi-Gul Shan without weapons and without a hope of survival.

CHAPTER 4

THE GATHERING STORM

SAKOLOV WAS the only soul in Shanghai who was excited about the arrival of the *Princess Wilhelmina*. Luxury liners came and went from the port daily, and yet Sakolov knew about the epoch-making importance of one its passengers.

"Welcome to Shanghai," Sakolov said when he shook the man's hand. The other man responded in Russian. The man was tall and well-built, with broad shoulders and a long, wiry beard. His eyebrows were similarly hirsute and gave his countenance an infernal appearance. He had a magnetic aura that seemed to enthrall Sakolov.

The two men got into a black taxi that sped off from the International Settlement. From the shadows, a Chinese man in a Western suit and hat appeared. The man walked to the nearest telephone. He dialed a familiar number.

"Yes?" said the voice on the other end of the line.

"Sakolov met someone from the *Princess Wilhelmina*. They are headed for the International Settlement. Please alert Agent Chow. I'll be at the station if he needs back-up." He placed the phone on the receiver. The man in the suit was Agent Fong, an experienced agent of the Special Branch.

For two months, his job had been to shadow Sakolov, and he had done his job well. The suspected communist agitator Sakolov never went anywhere in Shanghai without Agent Fong or the Special Branch following right behind him.

In the International Settlement, Agent Chow stood up from his chair at the café and made his way to the ringing telephone. He answered and learned that Sakolov was inbound. He nodded without saying a word. He paid his bill and made his way towards one of Sakolov's favorite haunts—Fuxing Park in the French Concession. Chow knew that Sakolov enjoyed reading in the park, and on occasion he gave political speeches that were attended by his fellow Russians.

Whereas Agent Fong was tall, well-dressed, well-groomed, and handsome, Agent Chow was short, fat, and slovenly. Agent Chow cared more about his nightly dinner and cups of oolong tea than his appearance His wife always nagged him about making a mess at home, and she also pestered him about mending his clothes or improving his rotten dental care. What Chow did not understand was how Fong, a bachelor, seemed to prefer primping and preening to chasing girls. There were plenty of single women in Shanghai, and Chow loved to watch them daily.

As for Sakolov, Chow had no doubt that the man was bankrolled by someone else. On paper, the Russian was a penniless drifter. And yet, both Fong and Chow shared notes about how the scruffy Russian always ate out and downed cups of tea at the Russian restaurants that had sprung up in the city since 1917. He did not seem to be hurting for money, even though Sakolov lacked a job. Chow wondered to himself if the stranger that Fong saw with Sakolov was the man's benefactor. "I might win an award for capturing these two Bolshevik agents," Chow said to himself. He smiled and patted his growing stomach at the knowledge that he would spend the award money on unforgettable feasts.

Chow's daydreaming came to an end when a black taxi stopped at the edge of the park and divulged two men, one of whom was the familiar Sakolov. Chow opened his notebook and scribbled notes about the date, time, and the general appearance of the other man. Chow walked confidently into the sunshine. He found a parallel path that allowed him to walk side-by-side with the two men, but from a safe distance. Chow observed Sakolov's animated conversation and wild gestures. He also noted that the other man remained stoic and mostly silent. The conversation remained one-sided until the men found a park bench. There, the unknown man began speaking. Chow, who found park bench within listening distance, could not make out a single word of the conversation, as it was conducted entirely in Russian. The unknown man spoke in a deep register. He spoke slowly too.

"The progress of our mission pleases me, Sasha." The man used the diminutive form of Sakolov's Christian name, and yet warmth and familiarity were missing from his tone.

"Yes. One-by-one, the enemy elements are crumbling," Sakolov responded.

"Morrison is dead."

"Yes."

"And your agents within the army have moved to take out Oppersdorff and Lucchini?"

"I know that my men are embedded in Oppersdorff's command. I also know that they moved out to Sichuan days ago. I cannot yet confirm that the deed has been done, though."

"When will you know?"

"I cannot say. Communication travels slowly in this country."

"The deadline must be met, Sasha. Do I need to remind you how important time is to our plans?"

"No, you do not need to remind me. I am working without sleep to make it happen. Trust me."

"And what about the book?"

Sakolov winced. The book was a topic that he did not like to discuss because it reminded him of his most recent failure.

"The book will be recovered soon. I know that it is currently in the possession of a policeman named Lewis. He is the man the SCMP have assigned to solve Morrison's murder. I know he took it from Marsh's room, but I do not know where he is keeping it. I already had his quarters searched."

"*Kurit'* failed?"

"He could not find the book, no."

"Pity."

"Shall we send him again?"

"I believe that we should be patient for the time being. The book is required for the ceremony. However, our forces are about to arrive. One half has already left Harbin, while the other is coming across the Pacific. Once we are at all full force, then we can take the book at the same time as we take the city. Have you made arrangements for our headquarters?"

"Yes. I used the money you wired me to bribe members of the Green Gang into leasing me own of their opium warehouses. It should be large enough."

"And what our friends, the communists?"

"I am meeting the editor of the *Shanghai Chronicle* this

evening to finalize plans. As for the weapons, I have been slowly collecting them and hiding them all across the city. The major shipment is still on track to arrive from Europe, as well. The local party cell has provided me with a list of names. They swear that the union men and party members can all be trusted to carry out the necessary work once the signal is given."

"Excellent. You have been far from flawless so far, Sasha, but I am pleased with the thrust of things."

"Will you attend the meeting tonight?"

"No. I have my own business to attend to. I will see you again very soon." At that the two men stood up, shook hands, and then departed. On a nearby bench, Agent Chow watched the two men leave. Once they were gone, he hurriedly wrote in his notebook about the three English words that he recognized: "Lewis" and "*Shanghai Chronicle*." Chow stood up from the bench and thought about his next move. His primary mission was to surveil Sakolov as part of the SCMP's complex mission to track and ultimately dismantle communism in the city. However, something that he could not quite describe compelled Chow to follow the other man instead. Maybe it was his bearing and air of importance, or maybe it the fact that the conversation clearly indicated that the other man was Sakolov's superior, but whatever the reason, Chow ran after the strange man as he walked further into the French Concession.

Unbeknownst to Chow or anyone else in Shanghai besides Sakolov, the other man had an infamous name and an even more hideous reputation. His name was Baron Konstantin von Allenstein, and he was not only a wanted criminal in Russia, Germany, and Austria, but he was also suspected of being the leader of a mysterious and reputedly evil group called the Secret Army of Abraxas.

To the best of anyone's knowledge, Allenstein was born in the Hapsburg empire to a Baltic German father and a mother of mixed German-Hungarian ancestry. His formative years were spent somewhere between Vienna and Graz, with his formal schooling was conducted at a private boarding academy in Switzerland. As a young man, Allenstein lived in Vienna, where he emersed himself in that city's occult milieu. For one moment in his strange chronology, Allenstein attempted to garner fame. He created a journal devoted to esotericism called *Ur* and crafted the flagship symbol and masthead himself. The select few who purchased the journal were taken aback by the stark images of chimeras, hydra-headed creatures, and giant salamanders that stood upright.

Ur gained a sinister reputation in Vienna and was promptly banned for promoting salacious and "un-Austrian" behavior by the city's populist mayor. Allenstein reacted to this development by disappearing from public view and becoming a recluse.

Because of his father's Russian citizenship, Allenstein was drafted into the officer corps as a member of the Imperial Guards. Allenstein cut an impressive figure in his uniform but proved to be an unreliable soldier. During his unit's first engagement, Allenstein went AWOL. He would not reappear again until the conflagration of 1917, when he came back to Petrograd announcing that he has the leader of a private force. His claims were laughed at by the Whites and Reds alike, who left Allenstein alone as a harmless crank. They were soon to learn the seriousness of Allenstein's assertions, for, during the winter of 1918, Allenstein seized the city of Omsk. Eyewitnesses who survived the massacre claimed that they saw a tall man on a horse leading an army dressed all in black. The army fell upon the Siberian city like a plague and consumed everything in its way. Churches were set alite. Graveyards were ruined and the dead interred. The Whites issued propaganda claiming that Allenstein's army was loyal to the Bolsheviks. In response, the Reds accused Allenstein of being a monarchist and in league with the equally odious "Mad Baron" Ungern-Sternberg.

During the month that Allenstein's army controlled Omsk, the city was ruled like a pirate's cove. All laws were rendered null and void. All marriages were dissolved, and Allenstein let his soldiers have their way with the city's women. Priests were put on trial and executed. Christians, Jews, and Mongols were gunned down in droves. Even Allenstein's co-ethnics were not sparred. Allenstein declared himself *khan* and hoisted his flag above every remaining building. The black banners with the blue-green skulls were how the shell-shocked country learned the name of the Secret Army of Abraxas.

Just as quickly as it appeared, the Secret Army of Abraxas vanished following a single battle with the Bolsheviks. Allenstein and his men ran off into the barren wastes of far-eastern Russia. The Bolsheviks, Whites, and Japanese all wanted Allenstein's force for their own purposes, but he and his men had successfully gone underground in order to wait for their next rising.

Chow followed Allenstein as he traversed the well-maintained and well-manicured streets of the French Concession. Of the entire International Settlement, Chow preferred the French Concession the most. Something in the Gallic temper made them lovers of beauty and aesthetics. Plus, as everyone in Shanghai knew, the French insisted on maintaining a separate government and municipal structure. Much to the chagrin of the British-domi-nated Shanghai Municipal Council, the French succeeded and flourished. Chow and his fellow Chinese were more at ease among the French than the Anglos, and as such he did not worry about disapproving stares or hushed tones as he followed the strange Russian.

Allenstein walked a zig-zagging path across the concession. He occasionally stopped at storefronts to admire the trinkets on display. He stayed the longest at one showcasing Russian baubles. Chow felt the onset of boredom as Allenstein failed to do anything exciting. The Special Branch agent was also hungry and felt guilty for not yet passing word to his fellow agents about either the meeting or Sakolov's suspected whereabouts. Chow stopped and made to turn in the opposite direction but ceased when he saw Allenstein's walking into *Le Dagon Rogue*. A cohort of the Jade Dragon in the English-speaking part of the International Zone, *Le Dagon Rogue* mostly counted among its customers Francophone expats and French officials spending two to three years in the city. Chow and everyone at the SMP knew that strange bar was a front for an opium den controlled by the Green Gang.

Le Dagon Rogue was popular with a higher caliber of addicts, as those connected to the drug trade and degenerate nightclub scene knew that the Green Gang only used the best quality opium from the Northwest Frontier at the bar. The bar also catered to other tastes by including prostitutes from Indochina, both male and female, for their customers. Chow only knew *Le Dagon Rogue* by reputation. He entered it behind Allenstein, who briefly spoke to a short, gray-haired Frenchmen before entering a backroom shaded by ermine curtains.

The man said something in French when Chow approached him. The agent tried at first to push past him, but the Frenchman proved to have an iron grip. He reiterated his earlier comment, but this time through gritted teeth. Chow showed him his SMP badge.

This loosened the man's grip, although not the scornful look in his eyes. He stood down and let Chow pass. From the corner of his eye, Chow saw the Frenchman make several frantic hand gestures to unseen individuals. This put the already nervous agent on guard. Still, Chow mustered up courage and followed the dark hallway of the bar's back portion. On each side were more ermine curtains. The curtains helped to maintain privacy in small cells that, judging by the smells and sounds that assailed Chow's nose, were used for either opium or lovemaking. Chow practically tip-toed to keep himself secret while the walls around him pulsated with sinful pleasures.

Chow found a flight of stairs located at a far wall. He took them slowly, as the stairs wound inward at a sharp angle. Chow never liked heights, so it made him uncomfortable to discover that the stairs led deep down into the bowels of the French Concession. The aroma of wet stone and the muffled noise of the city above indicated the depth of the secret chamber. Fear boiled up from Chow's stomach and encased his heart in a wall of anxiety. He kept a hold on his jacket's lapel as a weak attempt to steady himself.

His hands shook and his temples throbbed. Chow knew that he was in danger, and he knew death could come at any time. Still, duty remained paramount in his mind.

Eventually the stairs ended at a flat surface composed of large, rough stones. These stones were damp and slimy. Chow caught himself from falling several times. He shuddered to think what his fate would be if he fell and broke a leg in such a place. He main-tained a steady, but cautious pace in the darkened environment until, upon reaching yet another ermine gate, he stopped completely. He found that particular curtain contained decorative symbols. Chow studied them in the gloom. He could see from their barest outline that they were illogical puzzles that could not be identified or categorized. Some shapes resembled animals, especially marine animals like squids and octopi. Other symbols looked somewhat religious, although not of any religion that the Buddhist Chow recognized. Overall, the symbols perplexed and chilled Chow. Everything about *Le Dagon Rogue* seemed menacing.

Chow pulled apart the curtains and was shocked by the sudden appearance of light. The simple curtains had somehow managed to block out all the lit candles on the other side. The bedazzled Chow managed to count thirteen candles arranged in a large circle. Inside of the circle were individuals dressed only in simple cloths that covered their private parts. Chow saw that they were men and women, foreigner and Chinese. They swayed together and hummed in low tones together. Chow knew that he had stumbled onto some kind of ritual.

Outside of the candlelight circle were four others. Two were musicians—one playing a repetitive tone on a single drum, and the other a flutist blowing into a small and simple flute. Behind them, tall and imposing, was Allenstein. Allenstein was flanked by a much shorter Chinese man. To Chow's eyes, Allenstein's Chinese companion had the stereotypical appearance of a gangster, from his facial scar to his well-designed but gaudy clothing.

Two men watched the ritual with determination, but never joined in. The view seemed to give them satisfaction. As for Chow, he felt on the verge of a massive heart attack.

The special agent's discomfiture increased as the minutes passed, and the ritual grew louder. The supplicants swayed with greater intensity until, like dervishes, they became a blur of flesh and movement. The saliva in Chow's throat evaporated, and the sweat on his brow dried and turned into a kind of crust. Every particle in him was injected with fear, for some extrasensory part of him knew that the ritual and its strange attendees were connected to something evil.

At the exact same time, well to the north in Peking, Professor Georges Bruhl was startled by an unexpected movement in his study. The elderly gentleman looked up but found nothing amiss. Professor Bruhl lived in a plush domicile within Peking's Legation Quarter. His immaculate four-story house was full of incredible treasures from China and Europe. They were the result of a lifetime of travel and service to his small, but mighty nation. Professor Bruhl often chuckled to himself whenever he reflected on the fact that he owed his wealth and status to his diplomatic passport and his service to the king, and yet he had not set foot in Belgium since leaving Ghent at the age of sixteen in order to make his fortune in the Congo.

Now, in semi-retirement, Professor Bruhl spent his hours studying artifacts and amusing himself with books. Whatever work he did have came courtesy of General Fang. The general was the rare warlord of culture and learning, and he often passed curious relics off to Professor Bruhl in the hopes that the erudite Belgian could write a paper on them. "China is a land of ancient culture," General Fang would say in his halting French, "China may belong to barbarians at the moment, but that cannot last.

It is my duty to resurrect her greatness with her art, poetry, and history." Professor Bruhl did not like being lumped in with the "barbarians," but he agreed with the overall thrust of General Fang's mission. As such, when the general delivered to him a peculiar statuette found in the storage area of the city's museum, Professor Bruhl agreed to give it his full attention.

The statuette was on Professor Bruhl's desk that night when he got the strange sensation of being watched. The professor rose from his leather chair and examined the corners and crevices of his immense study. All he found were books—mountains of books in French, Dutch, German, Latin, and English. The books covered all manner of subjects, from geology to geography. Professor Bruhl planned on donating his library to the city of Peking upon his death, as the bachelor had no kin to give it to. Satisfied that there was nothing and nobody else in the study with him, Professor Bruhl turned back to his desk and its familiar leather chair.

"Who are you!" he shouted in Flemish. The target of his exclamation was the black-clad and lithe figure hunched over his desk. The masked figure had in its hands the strange statuette.

"Put that down this instant!"

The figure declined and moved closer to the study's waist-high window. Professor Bruhl moved to block the figure's path. The thing in black moved with cat-like speed. It struck the aged Belgian on the temple with the blade of his palm. The strike stunned Professor Bruhl, but he stayed in the fight. The old man had experienced his fair share of scrapes with unruly natives in the Congo, plus he had once traded bullets with Arab slavers while traveling by steamboat with several American mercenaries bound for the forts of the *Force Publique*. Professor Bruhl grabbed the golden letter opener from his desk and wielded it like a dagger. He thrust it towards the intruder, missing the figure's torso by inches. The move rendered Professor Bruhl exposed, and the figure kicked him swiftly in the nose.

The blow sent a dizzied Professor Bruhl to the floor. The black figure stood over the wounded academic and moved to deliver a killing blow. A raised black boot hovered over Professor Bruhl's face.

A knock interrupted the execution. A series of Mandarin words came from the other side of the study's door. Professor Bruhl recognized the voice of his beloved housekeeper, Mrs. Shan.

The panicked intruder absconded into the night with the statuette in his hands. Professor Bruhl tried to tell Mrs. Shan about what had happened to him, but the housekeeper could not understand his belabored moans. Professor Bruhl succumbed to unconsciousness before General Fang and his men arrived.

Back in Shanghai, when the bizarre statuette was removed from Professor Bruhl's desk, the ritual came to a sudden stop. The worshippers broke out into a loud and ecstatic cheer. Allenstein clapped his hands together, and the Chinese gangster struck up a cigar. Chow was puzzled by the sudden shift in attitude. Without realizing it, Chow relaxed his grip on the curtain. When he tried to correct it, he overcompensated, grabbed the hem of the curtain, and pulled it with a forceful tug. The curtains dropped to the cold stone. All eyes turned to him.

Allenstein shouted something in a foreign tongue and raised his finger at Chow. The supplicants rose and made chase as the outnumbered special agent raced for the stairs. Chow huffed and puffed and increased his speed until he finally placed his hand on the bottom of the staircase. He looked up and his heart sunk. There, a few steps above him, was the old Frenchman from earlier. Behind him were several men in white aprons. They all wielded butcher's blades like cleavers and steak knives. Chow turned back and saw that the semi-nude supplicants had already closed the distance. He had nowhere left to go.

· · ·

From the back of the crowd, Allenstein place his palms perpendicular to each other, slid them back and forth, and then closed them to make interlocking figures. At this signal, the supplicants attacked with unbridled fury. Like the Bacchae of Ancient Greece, they enjoyed the violence with a religious bloodlust. And like their forebearers, the supplicants used their bare hands to rend Chow to pieces.

CHAPTER 5
PRISONERS OF THE MOUNTAINS

THE DEEP DARKNESS and silence of the mountains unnerved Kenaghan. Still, the taciturn American handled the situation better than his compatriots. Bergstrom and Lucchini oscillated between whimpering and crying out against God and fate. Only Oppersdorff mirrored Kenaghan's calmness. The Prussian kept his electric torch leveled as the foursome trekked in the Sichuan night.

"What if there are more of them? What if they are following?" The panic in Bergstrom's voice was obvious.

"He's right. I think they are in the trees," Lucchini added.

Oppersdorff silenced both men. Kenaghan added by glaring at the Swede and Italian. Admittedly, he was frightened too. It was possible that the mutineers had followed them, and it was even more likely that the four would not last long in the wilderness. None had much beyond the clothes on their backs. Food was non-existent—a grave oversight in the original plan dreamed up by Oppersdorff and Lucchini.

.   .   .

"Why don't they just attack already? Get it over with!" Bergstrom was dangerously close to a nervous breakdown. This was never a good sign, and it was doubly bad because the four men had only been on their own for a few hours.

"If you insist on acting this way, Bergstrom, then you do not have to worry about the Chinese killing you. I will gladly do it myself," Oppersdorff barked. His threat silenced the Swede. However, fear hung over all four men like a thick vapor that could not be dissipated. Besides the possible presence of rifles and daggers, the men, especially Kenaghan and Oppersdorff, brooded about the Mi-Gul Shan. There were in the land of the Black Brotherhood, and though none were superstitious, all felt like an unwanted presence in the strange country. Overall, the atmosphere was bleak and was only becoming more so as the night wore on.

"China is the most populated nation on God's green earth. Surely, we will come to a village soon." Oppersdorff stopped and turned towards Bergstrom. He spoke to the Swede in a harsh whisper.

"Listen! Even if we stumble across a village, can you speak Mandarin? Hell, even Mandarin is unworkable in these hills. So, can you speak a local dialect? My guess is that you can do neither. Also, something tells me that you overlook the fact that we are not welcomed here, and locals are just as likely to turn on us as aid us."

"They could be cannibals," Lucchini answered. "Hunger always in these villages. We could be a banquet." Bergstrom put his hand to his throat to protect it from the suggested cannibals. Of all the white skins, his was the softest and most tender and therefore the most succulent.

"We all know that the situation is desperate. There is no reason to pretend otherwise. We are unarmed, hungry, and some of us are seriously wounded."

· · ·

Oppersdorff turned to Lucchini, whose arm still bled from underneath the grip of his free hand's palm. "But to give up, or to completely give into fear now is pointless. Yes, we may die, but we can die like men rather than skittish mice. What is your choice, Bergstrom?"

Bergstrom stayed silent. The conversation was over, so Oppersdorff returned to his position as the point-man. Kenaghan focused on staying alert. His ears were perked up for any extraordinary noise. This was no simple task; Kenaghan found rural China abuzz with strange sounds made by unfamiliar animals. He shivered at the thought of encountering one of the many varieties of venomous snakes known to East Asia, or worse, making contact with a hungry tiger in the dark. Kenaghan played through all the scenarios in his head.

As for Oppersdorff, his thoughts were solely on the best way to extract himself and his companions from their situation. As much as he had denounced the idea to Bergstrom, Oppersdorff still considered finding a nearby village their best option. Yes, it ran the risk of death, but it also included the possibility of salvation. Not all villagers and not all villages were prone to violence, Oppersdorff hoped. Lucchini was concerned with one thing: saving his bleeding arm and himself. Each step made the Italian airman feel dizzy, and he knew in his cloudy brain that that was a sure sign of blood loss. Death followed close at his side.

The four men walked in a staggered line. Their steps were halting and hesitant, as they had to rely on the light coming from Oppersdorff's torch. The light it provided was neither robust nor strong, and as such the inky blackness around them dominated. They were prisoners to the gloom, and more importantly they were captives to the weird world around them.

All four men jumped when they heard the noise.

"What in the world was that?" Bergstrom asked. He received no answer to his question. The air around them came alive with the strange caterwauling of an unseen and unknown beast. Even Kenaghan, the only one of the four with any serious experience with wild mountains, could not come up with a satisfactory explanation for the noise. It sounded to him like something between a large cat and a bird of prey. The scream was high-pitched and predatory polyrhythm. It moved across the night like a blade, and it warned each man that they were on the menu.

"I think it best if we find cover," Kenaghan suggested.

"Where? We're surrounded," Bergstrom said. Kenaghan knew that his old friend was right. There seemed to be no escape from the infernal cacophony. And yet the American thrust himself into action by grabbing Bergstrom by the arm and dragging him off of the narrow path and into the high grass all around them. "Get as flat as possible," he told Bergstrom. Both men went prone and prayed silently that their antagonists would fail to locate them.

Oppersdorff and Lucchini took a different tact. The Prussian wielded his electric torch like a searchlight. The yellow beam made random patterns in the air, but Oppersdorff failed to find anything. Nothing but a thick, impenetrable blackness greeted them. Yet even though nothing could be seen, all four felt but did not utter the obvious: they were being watched.

"I think whatever is out there has either retreated or means us no harm," Oppersdorff said unconvincingly. Before he could cajole Kenaghan and Bergstrom to leave their positions, the blackness around him came alive again. With an unbridled ferocity that seemed outside the capabilities of man, animal, or machine, a band of shadows struck Oppersdorff and Lucchini. The wound in the

Italian airman's arm was enlarged by unseen claws. The wound kept expanding until there was nothing left but a crimson stump of wet, pulpy sinew. Lucchini's instincts went to his arm.

His free hand shot out in a vain attempt to protect its damaged brother, but it was far too late. Worse, Lucchini's focus on his arm left him vulnerable elsewhere. The creatures of the night saw this, and many of their claws found Lucchini's throat. They ripped and pulled and tore until the Italian's head was removed from his body. The torso collapsed with a heavy thud on the Sichuanese dirt. The head briefly floated unattached before disappearing.

True to form, the battled-hardened Prussian turned to face his attackers. Oppersdorff barked curses in his native tongue while swinging his fists wildly. Sharp cracks indicated direct hits, which meant that the attackers were made of some kind of flesh after all. Oppersdorff's fists moved like pistons without cessation. A great amount of energy was expended, but the creatures learned to respect the Prussian's bravery.

"Come on you swine!" Oppersdorff bellowed in German. "I lived through Tannenberg and many Carpathian winters. Chinese black magic is nothing compared to a charging Russian horde. Come on and fight like men."

The weird attackers changed tact. They displayed intelligence by circling Oppersdorff and striking with quick jabs. Each blow was sharp and opened small cuts on the Prussian's body, but they were not fatal by themselves. This fact allowed to Oppersdorff keep fighting until the cuts became too numerous and he could not move his arms and legs without great pain and effort. He was too late in recognizing the strategy as the ancient Chinese torture of *lingchi*, or death by a thousand cuts. Exhausted and bleeding out rapidly, Oppersdorff dropped to his knees and looked towards the darkness. He smirked and whispered a prayer before the killing blow. Neither Kenaghan nor Bergstrom could hear his words.

What they did see was the heroic man's end—a gigantic swoosh of air went through the Prussian's sternum, thus cleaving him in two. The two halves collapsed simultaneously like a cow's carcass dropped accidentally from a meat hook.

"We need to run. We should have already been running," Kenaghan whispered to Bergstrom. The American could feel the Swede shaking beside him. Thanks to that nervous energy, Bergstrom stood up and ran off into the night with great speed. Kenaghan struggled to follow him and push away the brush at the same time. Each stride layered upon the next, as Kenaghan felt the sticky hot night cling to his already sweat-soaked uniform. He could only hear Bergstrom, and yet somehow, maybe because of their long friendship, Kenaghan knew that Bergstrom would head towards the north. The debauched Swede was still a Viking, Kenaghan knew, and for him North was home.

The race into the strange wilderness continued for uncounted minutes until, with a speed reminiscent of the attack on the doomed Lucchini and Oppersdorff, Kenaghan heard Bergstrom cry out. The scream was a mixture of surprise and horror. The ground beneath him gave Kenaghan no time to ponder Bergstrom's predicament. The pair had fallen off a short hill or cliff and began tumbling ever downward. Neither man felt every revolution; both were left unconscious well before their bodies stopped moving.

———

Kenaghan cursed as soon as he awoke. Every part of his body pulsated with pain. Everything hurt—his head, his arms, his legs, and his back. For a moment, Kenaghan worried that the fall had paralyzed him. This fear evaporated when he managed to move his fingers and toes. From there it was long, arduous task to raise himself to a seated position.

. . .

Kenaghan felt his brains swim uncontrollably. The drastic fall had left him not only bruised but dizzy. He was forced to hold back vomit as he made small and slow head movements. He celebrated the fact that he was still alive, but the old soldier knew that he still had a battle ahead of him.

A battle without Bergstrom.

Kenaghan called the Swede's name but received no reply. The night was still dark and silent all around him. Kenaghan called and called again. Still nothing. Even the crickets stayed mute to the American's pleas. The situation seemed hopeless, but Kenaghan pressed on. He had no other choice. He got himself to a standing position and began shambling forwards. His right foot dragged behind him, indicating a serious injury of some sort. Kenaghan placed the pain in a separate compartment of his mind. The rest was dedicated to survival and finding Bergstrom. He limped on in the dry grass and over rocks that dug into the small cracks in his damaged boots. Kenaghan did his best to forget about what he had seen before the fall, but he could not help but worry about the unseen threats around him. What were those things that had so easily eviscerated Lucchini and Oppersdorff? Kenaghan prayed that they were tigers or possibly an as-yet undiscovered species of mammal. He hoped that they were anything but what the darkest part of his mind suspected—the Mi-Gul Shan.

Kenaghan's thoughts were interrupted by the surprising glow directly ahead of him. The glow appeared to be a strange mixture of yellow and green. While the color was unfamiliar, its dancing cadence indicated that it was fire—that primordial substance of succor and fear since the earliest days of mankind. A fire meant people, and people meant safety. Or at least more safety than the forest, Kenaghan thought. He walked slowly and lightly towards the glow. He recognized but did not dwell on the fact that the forest around him seemed to grow blacker the nearer he got to the light. It was unnatural, he knew, and yet nothing in China had ever seemed natural to the American.

Kenaghan found the light and its source. A small bonfire ringed with black stones stood in a small clearing. Kenaghan crept towards the light and found it cold. The flame did not give off any warmth, nor did it provide comfort. Indeed, for the first time that night, Kenaghan shivered. The source of the chill was the cave, which was directly behind the fire. Kenaghan thought to himself that the fire's author was likely in the cave. A hermit of some sort. He knew that such men lived all over rural China, especially in the mostly untraveled mountains of Sichuan. Kenaghan also thought that the shelter of the cave was the most likely hiding spot for Bergstrom, his friend who never passed up an opportunity to secure creature comforts for himself.

"Ingemar! Ingemar!" Kenaghan rarely used Bergstrom's Christian name. He shouted it until he was hoarse. There was no answer. Yet, Kenaghan did not give up the idea that his friend had fled into the cave. He entered the darkness after fashioning a makeshift torch made from grass and the eerie fire. Kenaghan's torch would not last long, but he knew that it was better than total darkness.

The cave had a fetid stench that Kenaghan could not describe. In many ways it smelled like the battlefields of the Great War. Water was not the only cause of the cave's dampness, as Kenaghan opened his mouth to breathe and tasted the familiar coppery consistency of blood. Many things had bled and bled a lot in that cave. Kenaghan prayed that the deaths had been animals. He shuddered to think that one of the bleeders may have been Bergstrom.

"Ingemar! Hello?" Kenaghan voice echoed all over the cave's

walls. The cave seemed to go on forever into the darkened void, almost as if it was the hollow interior of an entire mountain range.

"The Black Brotherhood," Kenaghan whispered to himself. The memory of Oppersdorff's fairy tale caused his heart to race and his mind to panic. It did not matter whether or not Kenaghan believed in the superstitions of Chinese peasants; the mere idea that something was amiss in the forest, which the local villagers surely believed, was enough to frighten the hard man.

The fact that Kenaghan had not yet located Bergstrom also terrified him. Every instinct told him to turn around, and yet Kenaghan pressed on, going further and further into the cave as the last pieces of grass burned to ash. Eventually there was nothing but darkness. Kenaghan bellowed out one last call for his friend.

Then, from somewhere in the stygian blackness, a low rumbling emerged. At first it sounded like thunder. Kenaghan thanked what little luck he had left from saving him from the rain. But then the rumbling began to pulsate, almost as if the entire cave was a giant's lung. Kenaghan felt the vibrations in his tattered boots. He knew that something, or somethings, were alive and near. In desperation, Kenaghan outstretched his hands and used his fingers to examine the air. He at least wanted to know where his enemies were coming from, for Kenaghan knew instinctively that whatever was in the cave with him was imbued with sheer malice. Kenaghan's fingertips felt nothing but the damp air until a warm vapor, almost like a breath, marched over his hand. A pungent and rancid smell arose as Kenaghan let out a war whoop and prepared to defend himself. No fight came; no battle joined. Instead, from out of the far depths of the cave came a series of shrill cries. They emanated from a human throat. They had the awful cadence of torture. It was as if the cave had transmogrified into a dungeon from the twelfth century. Kenaghan listened to them until, flush with terror, he ran screaming out of the cave.

Kenaghan would run until he collapsed due to exhaustion. There, on the outskirts of a nameless Chinese village, the veteran of some battles, laid down to die.

What had driven him to madness was recognition. Kenaghan not only knew the cries were human but knew that they were the final exclamations from his dying friend.

CHAPTER 6
UNNAMABLE HORRORS

INSPECTOR LEWIS FOUND it impossible to endure an entire shift at the stationhouse. Everyone, even the usually stoic Sikh guards, were full of mourning for the death of Agent Chow. Inspector Lewis had never interacted with the Special Branch man prior to his demise, but he knew that Chow was popular with his comrades. Men spent hours praising Chow in their own tongues while occasionally dabbing their eyes. The Chinese officers were the most distraught of all. Lewis had grown to distrust elaborate displays of grief from the Chinese. He knew that such outpourings of emotion were part of saving face, and yet he could not help but feel that the grief for Chow was sincere.

The way that Chow had died made things worse. The tough and savvy agent had been completely eviscerated by unknown assassins, some of whom had feasted on his flesh. Then, after murdering him, the killers had simply dumped his body like so much trash in one of the Chinese districts of the city. A humble beggar alerted had alerted the SMP. The responding officers—two veteran patrolmen generally immune to the random cruelties of Shanghai, had both retched upon seeing Chow's remains. It was all any officer could talk about. Mixed in with the sadness was a thirst for revenge.

Lewis felt no pity for the murderers, but he also did not like thinking about the fate that awaited them in the bowels of some prison or stationhouse after their capture. Because he had no connection to the case, Inspector Lewis decided to spend the gloomy day following up with Johansen.

He found the Norseman at the SVC barracks. Johansen rose to greet him with a handshake. It was noticeably less firm and assured than normal.

"Everything alright," Lewis asked?

"Frankly, no. Today the heavens have fallen, and I have felt every blow. First of all, as you well know, the murder of Special Agent Chow has put all of the security forces on high alert. Simple murder is one thing, but such a brutal murder directed an officer of the law is another matter entirely. Some fear that it is a prelude to an uprising."

"Communists?"

"They would be the most likely suspects. And if the specter of a Bolshevik massacre is not bad enough, our own Intelligence Division just released a memo today outlining the growing threat of Japanese espionage within the city. It seems that Tokyo has plans on either occupying the city outright or bombing it to smithereens with their new ships and planes. The memo makes quite a convincing case that a Japanese incursion is not only possible but likely within the year."

"That means more drill for me, then?"

"Naturally. I find it blackly comical that any move by the Japanese would be done under the banner of protecting the city from the Reds. So, if we really are on the precipice of a Bolshevik revolution, then Tokyo would be our salvation and our destroyer. You know as well as I that our samurai friends have no desire to let our strange European colony continue on in peace and prosperity."

"Crime or war. Or both."

"Yes. And then we have the issue of that damnable book. *Unaussprechlichen Kulten.* Have you any idea what you forced me to read?"

"None whatsoever."

"Well, my friend, this tome should never cross the desk of someone prone to fits of mania. Only those of sound mind and solid faith should ever crack its spine. Even then I would warn them away."

"I never thought you would be prone to superstitions, Johansen."

"I am not. I am not confessing that I believe the contents of this book. Rather I am merely admitting that the author, von Junzt, had a captivating pen. The man clearly believed in what he was writing about, and therefore any mentally deficient or asocial types would fall for this pabulum quite easily."

Lewis could not hide his growing interest. "And pray, what is the book about."

The hardy Norwegian sat up straight in his chair and cleared his throat. He also made sure that his light blue eyes connected with and held the attention of Lewis's green ones.

"The book purports to be an exhaustive examination of the secret cults of the world. Not only that, but the mad German recreated ancient maps, deciphered hieroglyphs, and interpreted antediluvian statuary, or at least what he thought was antediluvian statuary, in order to exhaust his poor readers with greater and greater evidence of his central thesis."

"Which is?"

"Von Junzt believed that there were gods on Earth before Jehovah and before Allah. These gods had names like Ghatan-othoa, Ghisguth, and Hziulquoigmnzhah. These gods had loyal worshippers. The first adherents were the inhabitants of Earth before the arrival of humans. Early man worshipped these gods until something cataclysmic happened.

Von Junzt is coy about what this cataclysm was, but he gives hints that it might have been the arrival of a gigantic meteor. If true, then von Junzt's account of early human development enjoys an idiosyncratic chronology not shared by any serious scientist or theologian, here or in Europe. The late author also believed that the first, pre-human worshippers somehow managed to survive despite the encroachment of mankind. One can find them if they really want to."

"Alright, where do we look and when should we start," Lewis said with an impish grin.

"We can start right here in China, or *Cathay* as our great-grandparents used to say. Von Junzt dedicates a few paragraphs to gruesome mountain creatures in Sichuan called the Mi-Gul Shan. Seems they are giant salamander demons who prefer the taste of human blood. Von Junzt records they are a warrior race prone to violence, especially against those who trespass into their domains. As far as religion goes, the Mi-Gul Shan worship their ancestor, the original salamander deity named Uexll. He has much to say about their powers, especially their ability to blend in with whatever scenery they find themselves in. They're not shapeshifters, but they're close. Thankfully, our German friend records that they are loathe to leave the "Black Brotherhood," which is the local name for a series of mountains in Sichuan. They get homesick easily, it seems. Either way, I would not want to mess with them or the parrot monsters that the book talks about. Gives me the shivers.

"My overall opinion," Johansen said while putting the book back down on his desk, "is that if this book is somehow connected to a crime in Shanghai, then the previous owner or owners was a student of the occult. That is the only reason why anyone would have a book like this. Well, unless they are actual believers and practitioners. In that case they would need a psychoanalyst, not you."

"I appreciate the confidence. Thanks for generously donating your time to this volume, too. Your contributions to the safety and security of Shanghai will not be forgotten," Lewis winked at Johansen.

"Your disregard for basic military bearing and decorum is astounding to me, sergeant." Johansen winked back at his friend as the two shared a laugh. With that they shook hands. Lewis left the barracks and made his way to his hotel. His plan was to write down Johansen's findings, then move onto investigating Sakolov. So far, not much had turned up on Marsh besides what Lewis had discovered at the crime scene. Morrison's funeral had come and gone, and Lewis still could not tell the dead man's relatives much. Did not seem to matter; all most of them cared about was the contents of the late businessman's will. Lewis's other target, Sakolov, had seemingly gone underground. Although whispers around the stationhouse hinted at the fact that Agent Chow had been part of the permanent detail assigned to the suspected Bolshevik, Special Branch would not confirm anything to the Homicide Division or Inspector Lewis. Inter-departmental rivalries never stopped, even for murder.

Lewis walked the several blocks back to his hotel room. Inside, instead of his usually neat room, Lewis found a disheveled and disorganized mess. Someone had completely trashed it. He found his mattress on the floor, all of his dresser drawers open and emptied, and his toiletries scattered pell-mell all over the bathroom. It was a mess. Lewis demanded an explanation from the hotel staff, but none was forthcoming. No one had requested access to his room, nor had the maids entered it at any point throughout the day.

"Any suspicious characters lingering around my floor?" Lewis had asked.

The reply he received in turn was as unexpected as it was honest: "Everyone in Shanghai is suspicious," the hotel manager had said in textbook Mandarin. Lewis affirmed the truth of the man's statement. He spent the rest of the day grumbling and cleaning his room. "Some detective work I have done today," he said after the sun sank and he finally found himself with presentable quarters.

That same night, elsewhere in the Foreign Concession, Johansen settled down into his usual routine. He lit his pipe and let the sweet-smelling cherry tobacco overtake him. His wife, Greta, sat busily playing solitaire in the kitchen. Like her husband, she too had a routine, which was one last cup of black coffee before bed. The caffeine never affected her. Johansen could not say the same. Sleep had never been his friend, and on days when he had one cup too many, he did not even bother to touch his bed.

Great wished her husband a good night at ten p.m. Johansen kissed her lightly on the cheek. He promised that he would be upstairs to join her soon. In truth, Johansen had several worries on his mind. The intelligence reports were first and foremost. The Norwegian knew that a Red revolt could easily cripple the city. Shanghai had been a powder keg for years, what with the communists, Nationalists, and Japanese all constantly maneuvering to take control. Then there was always the anger and resentment. Johansen had lived in the city long enough to feel the hatred the average Chinese felt for the Westerners in their midst. All the guns, tanks, and planes of the SMP and the SVC would not be able to defeat a popular uprising, let alone a full-scale invasion from Tokyo.

The damnable tome by von Junzt also weighed heavily on his mind. The hours he had spent reading about secret rites and infernal monstrosities had bothered him more than he cared to admit. The typically hardy and reserved Norsemen found himself having daydreams about twilight grottos full of cavorting cultists and their blasphemous shrines.

He saw their eldritch gods with his mind's eye, and he hated every minute of it. Still, he could not stop his mind from wandering to the darkest places. At one point he envisioned a figure clad all in black, with a black mask and the lithe but powerful body of a jungle cat. The figure moved in smoke or fog, almost as if it had arrived on Earth from the hottest portions of Hades. Johansen could not name the entity, but he knew it originated from the feverish mind of von Junzt. Fear turned to horror as Johansen slowly recognized that he was not dreaming or drifting off to sleep. The figure that he saw was in reality standing right above his chair.

"Faen!" he cursed as the creature reached out to strangle him. Johansen grasped the figure's hands and tried to pry them loose from his throat. The slender figure had a grip of iron. Johansen resorted to kicking it, punching it, and even biting its hand in order to loosen its stranglehold. Johansen exhausted himself, but eventually managed to temporarily escape the entity's clutches. His first move of offense was to throw his still smoldering pipe at the creature's face. This did no damage, but it caused enough distraction for Johansen to leave his chair and take up a more advantageous position. The Norwegian found a letter opener near-by and held it out before him. He told the entity to leave his home immediately or face the possibility of death. The creature said nothing in return. Johansen felt it staring through his flesh and into his soul. Yet, Johansen could not see its eyes, for the entity was darker than the night outside of Johansen's windows.

The Norwegian cursed the creature and attempted to move into the den that connected his sitting room with the kitchen. The creature followed every step in a dangerous game of pantomime. As Johansen moved to enter the den, the creature stopped. Johansen braced himself for one last battle. He fully expected the figure in black to pounce on him. Instead, the dark shape turned and headed upstairs.

"Greta!" Johansen shouted. He raced up the stairs, trailing behind the fast-moving specter the whole time. He continued to shout his wife's name until he felt his throat constrict. Inside of the bedroom that he shared with his wife; Johansen found the figure hovering just above his wife's face. It was the position of the incubus—the tormentor of female slumber. The angle and height of the creature's position indicated that it was not human. Johansen did not care; he threw himself onto the entity and fought as fiercely as a lion. The Norwegian soldier stabbed wildly with the letter opener. He felt it impact, and yet his antagonist never moaned or whimpered. The furious blows, which would have caused a normal man to bleed profusely, produced nothing. Johansen kept stabbing and kept fighting.

Greta awoke in horror. The middle-aged woman, who had grown up safe and secure as the daughter of a Christiania banker, saw true danger for the first time in her life. She found her husband wrestling with a dark figure at the foot of her bed. She heard him struggle. She heard him fight for every breath. She saw the metal letter opener in his hands, and she saw him stab his opponent several times.

"Per! Please stop," Greta cried. Her confused brain saw visions of her beloved husband arrested and tried for murder. She would be then left all alone in a strange city—a city she never wanted to live in in the first place. Johansen never responded to her calls. He kept fighting until his arms gave up from exhaustion. She saw his chest rise and fall like a balloon being inflated and deflated. Her Per was too tired to block the final blows, which crashed upon his head and chest with swift violence. The black figure slashed Johansen's face, causing one of his eyeballs to leave its socket and hang down the mortally wounded man's cheek.

The next blow split open the Norwegian man's mouth. The final and killing blow severed his throat in two. The brave Johansen, one of the most invaluable men of Shanghai, died choking on his own blood from multiple lacerations. Each wound bore the distinct three-fingered pattern of the entity's claws.

Greta never got the chance to learn more about her husband's assailant. She was fortunate enough to faint from fright. She never saw her husband's final moments, nor did she feel anything when the entity pressed its sharp thumb right through her windpipe.

Lewis and the rest of Shanghai would not know about these events for another two days. There was one individual who knew well in advance, though. Indeed, he knew of the events even before their completion. From his secret chambers beneath *Le Dagon Rogue*, Allenstein congratulated *Kurit'* for another successful operation. However, the Russian was dissatisfied that his familiar failed once again to find the book. Allenstein knew that the hour was growing late, and the book was an essential piece of his plans.

Still, Allenstein knew that the book would not evade him forever. And best of all, his forces were already gathered and preparing to strike. The chaos would provide the perfect cover to find the book, and with the book in his possession, Allenstein could harness the power of the Menagerie for eternity.

The Russian smiled.

"MY GOD, how many is that now?" Inspector Lewis asked Sergeant Grant.

"Too damn many."

The men stood over the corpse of a homeless man. For well over a month, the streets of Shanghai had been littered with the corpses of unknown individuals. Someone or something was picking apart the city's homeless population, one by one. Each murder was more outrageous than the last. Acts of cannibalism and necrophilia were common indicators that it was the handiwork of Agent Chow's assassin. Lewis and the entire SMP were at the end of their tethers. Few if any of them were sleeping at night.

The murders hit Lewis especially hard. He was a lost man in many different ways. After months of no action or leads, his investigation into the murder of Hugh Morrison had stalled and was on the cusp of becoming a cold case. That meant that the case would be out of his hands. While it frustrated him to no end, Lewis knew that he could crack it. He operated with the germ of a theory, which included the idea that Morrison was involved in some kind of cult alongside Marsh, the Bolshevik Sakolov, and the military advisors Oppersdorff and Luchini.

What connected all of them was the accursed book by von Junzt—the same book that tied poor Per Johansen to the case as well. That was an idea that Lewis kept to himself and dared not speak aloud. Most of all, the detective blamed himself for introducing his friend to the tome and thereby getting him involved in something diabolical. Clarity had come to Lewis at the crime scene.

It was a hotter than normal day in Shanghai, which had caused Johansen's body to swell and ooze. Lewis managed to maintain enough composure to fully examine the bodies of Per and Greta Johansen. Like the other officers, Lewis left convinced that the couple had been mauled by the same individual as Agent Chow. Unlike the others however, Lewis was convinced that the killer was something other than a mere man. He felt his last traces of rationality leave him when he began reading from the *Unaussprechlichen Kulten*. The book's contents merged with the facts of the Morrison-Johansen cases. The use of the strange dagger to kill Morrison and the presence of three-fingered claw marks on the corpses of the Johansens convinced Lewis that something beyond the pale was afoot. The idea grew stronger when, out of the blue, a man named Professor Bruhl called for him.

The short, bespectacled professor had entered Lewis's office at the worst possible time. The inspector's desk was riddled with crime scene photos, notes, and more memos than he cared to read. Also on the desk was von Junzt's book. Professor Bruhl bypassed introductions and picked up the tome.

"Where did you get this?" he asked in Mandarin. The scholar knew that SMP officers only advanced to Lewis's position if they could converse in the language, but Bruhl switched to a more comfortable English when he saw the look of shock on the lawman's face.

"Who the devil are you?"

"My name is Bruhl. I have come down from Peking because I believe that I can help the Shanghai police. And my aid concerns the very same contents as this terrible book."

Bruhl put the book back down on Lewis's desk. He next seated himself and lit a cigarette. After the first puff of smoke left his lips, he began to speak.

"I am not normally a man interested in the horrors of everyday life, Inspector Lewis. I prefer to pursue knowledge then worry about who is killing whom. It is the East, after all. However, a series of strange events, in addition to these rash of murders in Shanghai, have convinced me to pay attention. I will start with what happened to me first."

Bruhl offered Lewis a cigarette, which the latter declined. The professor enjoyed a few more puffs while starring out the window directly behind Lewis. It was a cloudy day. Gray days were becoming more common in the city, almost as if the clouds were gathering from all across China for something troublesome.

"I was attacked one night in my study. My home is in the Legation Quarter in Peking. I am close personal friend and advisor to General Fang. I do not say this to brag, but to underscore that only the insane would try and attack me in my own home. I am also a man with a history of violence, sir. But this...thing...attacked without fear. It also had a singular mission. You see, I am something of a collector of oddities. People all across the north know this, and many times peasants and scholars alike call upon me to inspect some curio or other. One item was given to me by the city museum of Peking, who figured it would do better in my collection than in the rubbish bin.

"The item is a small, hand-sized statuette. It was apparently created by a mad peasant from Sichuan who claimed to have seen the object in real life. I once found this impossible to believe, for the statuette shows a type of hybrid, half-man and half-animal, reminiscent of Ancient Egypt.

"Yet it is an instinctively loathsome figure—a slimy salamander god with no mouth. The sculptor spent his final years in a lunatic asylum, as he should have. This, Inspector Lewis, is what the figure wanted when it attacked me. It got it too."

"And you believe this attack has something to do with our crime wave in Shanghai?"

"Yes. I doubt you will believe me, but my studies have forced me to conclude that it is true. You see, I know that the figure that attacked me was not human."

"An animal?"

"No. A spirit. A type of wraith. A demonic entity called a familiar. Such creatures have existed for aeons in Western occultism, and most associate them with black cats and witches. The truth is that familiars can take on any shape or form. It depends on the magical powers of their owner. The more adept the conjurer is, the more powerful and capable their familiar. This familiar almost killed me, thus indicating a mage of immense power.

"I learned all of this from the *Necronomicon*, the *Book of Eibon*, and the *G'harne Fragments*. I also read a partial translation of the book which is on your desk at this very moment. All of them spoke of similar things, including secretive cults lead by undead mages who can control entire armies of familiars if they wish. These cults get their power from blood, or more importantly the spilling of blood."

"Are you suggesting that such a cult is at work in Shanghai?" Lewis asked. At some point he had reached for one of Bruhl's proffered cigarettes. He was smoking it at a furious pace.

"Indeed I am. Look at the murders that you have recently suffered and continue to suffer: all poor indigents mutilated. They are found with their entire lifeforce, their blood, splattered in every direction, as if the killer or killers seek to dampen the city's soil with plasma. Then there are the murders of the unfortunate Agent Chow and that Norwegian family."

Inspector Lewis's heart sank at the mention of his friend Per Johansen. Even more troubling was the fact that Bruhl, a veritable stranger, had placed the deaths of Chow and the Johansen family in the same category as the homeless murders.

"From what I understand, Agent Chow was partially eaten."

"Yes."

"And the Johansens both had wounds in a sort of three-fingered pattern, yes?"

"How did you know that?" Lewis said while pounding his fist on his desk. No one, not the papers nor the SMP leadership, had published that information. The select few who knew it were Lewis and the other homicide detectives.

"I said before that I am an official in the government of General Fang, and the general has spies everywhere. Shanghai is the jewel prized above all else in China, and General Fang wants it."

Inspector Lewis twisted in his chair. He did not have strong feelings about General Fang or the government in Peking. Indeed, like most Westerners, he was more inclined towards the northern warlords than the southern ones, for the Nationalists never hid their desire to destroy the International Settlement. Still, the idea that the SMP was filled with Fang's spies made Lewis deeply uncomfortable.

"But I am not here as a representative of General Fang. I am here to offer my help. I believe that I can aid you and the police in your search for the killer." Bruhl opened the leather satchel that he had brought with him. He pulled out several volumes of ancient age. "These books contain all manner of spells and counter-spells. There are several that explicitly deal with thwarting wraiths, even ones as powerful as the one that attacked me and seems to be killing your people."

Lewis thumbed through the pages. He could not understand a word, as each tome was either written in Latin, Greek, or Hebrew. Bruhl told him not to worry, for he was adept at all three languages.

"We really should not waste any more time, Inspector. It will be a full moon tonight. We cannot let that kind of power rot away."

"What do you propose to do?"

Bruhl handed Lewis a slip of paper. On it was written an address.

"Meet me at my quarters this evening just before sunset. I will have everything arranged. You do not have to bring anything other than a willingness to cooperate. It will appear strange and maybe even a little dangerous to you but trust me: I believe it will work."

With that, the professor stood up and shook the policeman's hand. He left the station without saying another word. Lewis took seconds just pondering what the odd man had said. A large part of him outright rejected the idea that a specter was going around killing people in the city, including his good friend and his wife. But another, much darker part of him accepted the possibility. Strange things had indeed been happening for months and top it all was the fact that Lewis remained completely stumped. At the very least, Bruhl offered something new and novel about the case. Maybe he could help, Lewis reasoned.

Hours later, just as dusk began to coat Shanghai in an amber gloom, Lewis arrived at the address that Bruhl had given him. It was a rather plush home built in the Chinese style and located in a part of the city under Chinese law. Lewis stuck out like a sore thumb, as Westerners, even police officers on their beats, preferred to avoid wandering into the Chinese sections of the city. Lewis's knocks were answered by a Japanese servant. The man was dressed immaculately in the familiar custom of an English manservant. The contrast took Lewis aback, but he nevertheless followed the man deeper into the well-lit quarters. There, in the sitting room, was Bruhl.

"Inspector Lewis! Thank you so much for coming. You may go now, Kenji. I will no longer require your services tonight." The Japanese butler bowed and exited the room. He moved so silently that Lewis could not even hear his footfalls.

"Good. We will not be disturbed tonight," Bruhl said.

"Wouldn't it be wiser to have someone else here in case your hoodoo goes haywire?" Lewis asked in jest.

"No," Bruhl said in all seriousness. "Besides, Kenji could not help us. I rather suspect he would not aid us even if he could. You see, Kenji is only playacting as my servant. He is actually a member of the Japanese military police. My dear general sent him down here to keep an eye on me. Right now, Kenji is off on his other mission for his true master, that being Tokyo of course."

Lewis shook his head at the labyrinthine intrigues of his adopted city. Someday historians will look back on this epoch and go mad, he thought to himself as Bruhl escorted him deeper into the home. Eventually he stopped at a sliding door made of paper.

"Beyond this door will be things that may frighten you. Or you may scoff. Either way, I think that we will move one step closer to solving our shared problem if we do everything according to the ritual. Please just follow my instructions as I tell them to you."

Bruhl pulled the screen aside. Inside was a room illuminated by rings of candles, some white, some black, and others red. In the center was a pentacle made of salt. Ringed along the edges were characters of unknown origin. Lewis felt an instinctual loathing for the scene. Yet, Bruhl's assurances comforted him somewhat. Before long he found himself on his back in the middle of the circle. Bruhl handed him a vial that contained some kind of ointment.

"Are you a religious man, Inspector Lewis?"

"Not particularly."

"Were you perhaps raised in the Catholic tradition as a child?"

"No. My family are Anglicans. Simple, plain Anglicans."

"I see. Well, I was raised Catholic, so the first part of this ritual will be natural for me. Please just follow along." Bruhl opened the vial and dabbed several drops of the ointment on the fingers of his right hand. He then made the sign of the cross. Lewis followed suit in an almost perfect imitation (some of the ointment splashed on his shirt collar). Bruhl seemed satisfied.

"Excellent. The next step is to close your eyes and clear your mind. Your eyes must be absolutely shut and your mind completely blank. The ritual cannot proceed otherwise. My advice is to mimic the sleep state to the best of your ability without fully falling asleep. Do you understand?"

"Yes."

"Good. Let us begin."

Lewis closed his eyes and tried to clear his mind. It proved hard to erase all of his thoughts, for the bizarre circumstances clouded his thoughts. Still, Lewis fought hard to wrest control of his thoughts. At the same time, Professor Bruhl began a hypnotic chant that barely moved above a whisper. The words were indistinct and unknown to Lewis, and he found it impossible to place the language. It sounded nothing like English or Mandarin, and Lewis failed to place it as either Latin or Greek.

Unbeknownst to the hardboiled detective, Professor Bruhl had begun the ancient Saaamaaa Ritual. The origins of the ritual were shrouded in mystery, with many claiming that its origins in the fabled city of Atlantis. Bruhl had discovered it in the forbidden city of Lhasa. Following a successful incursion by General Fang and his allies, Bruhl has been awarded the company of a Tibetan priest. Nominally a Buddhist, the priest was in actuality an adept magician with an encyclopedic knowledge of the occult. It was he who had first taught Bruhl the ritual after months of serious warnings about the ritual's power. That night in Shanghai was Bruhl's first performance of the Saaamaaa Ritual.

Despite Bruhl's admonition, Lewis found it impossible to fend off sleep. The sandman took control of his eyes and body, plus Bruhl's soft-throated chanting lulled the exhausted detective into slumber. Within seconds Lewis began having the most vivid dreams. These dreams disturbed him, for Lewis was not a man prone to dreams of any sort, let alone the nightmares that assailed him. Lewis saw himself trapped on a boat in the middle of a black ocean. A hot, piercing rain lashed against his skin, and Lewis felt every droplet. The boat rocked to and fro with great violence, and all around it was limitless black sea. Lewis found himself alone—a shipwrecked

Ancient Mariner seemingly adrift on Styx. He felt nothing but panic.

The sky began to open up in the dreamworld. Lewis saw with growing horror a small circle of red widen until, as if pulling apart a curtain, a creature darker than the sea emerged. Smoke followed behind it, thus convincing Lewis that he was seeing nothing less than Satan himself emerging up from the bowels of Hell. The infernal entity crept closer to Lewis's simple boat. It blasphemously mimicked Christ by walking on the black water in order to approach the petrified police officer. As it got closer, Lewis's nostrils filled up with the smells of fire, brimstone, and decay. The pungent scent got so bad that Lewis began to gag. This gaging turned into retching, which forced the sleeper awake.

To his horror, Lewis opened his eyes to see the same creature from his dream standing just beyond the protective circle. He could not control the screams that escaped from his throat.

"You fool!" Bruhl raised himself to a standing position. Without warning he flung the vial at the creature. The ointment caused the creature's black-as-pitch skin to blister and burn. The smell was atrocious, but not as awful as the entity's high-pitched screams. Lewis placed his hands over his ears to block at the screams. Undaunted, Bruhl began chanting anew, this time he was as loud as humanely possible. The singing caused the creature to shriek even louder.

"Stop it! My God, my ears are going to bleed!" Lewis shouted. His pleas had no effect on Bruhl, who continued his chanting until the creature buckled and sank to the floor in obvious pain.

Realizing that the hour of victory was imminent, Bruhl breathed deeply, picked up a handful of the salt from the protective circle, and blew it all over the demonic familiar. He bellowed one last word: the final banishment decree of the Saaamaaa Ritual.

The result was instantaneous. Like a flash of lightning in the dark, the entity glowed for a second before disappearing altogether.

After a minute of silence, Lewis spoke: "What in God's name just happened?"

"An imperfect ritual," Bruhl said, "but we achieved the desired result, nonetheless. I must admit that I did not expect that last bit to work, but it did."

"What did you do?"

"What we did, my friend, was send that familiar back to its maker. It was a strong beast, and if its wizard is of equal power, then both will soon expire. However, if the wizard is of great strength, then he will be injured, possibly even crippled, but will remain alive. The familiar will be no more, no matter what."

At precisely the same time as Bruhl spoke to Lewis, Sakolov ran as fast as he could to his master's chambers inside the depths of *Le Dagon Rouge*. A series of anguished cries had alerted him to some kind of trouble. There, in the gloomy quarters favored by Allenstein, Sakolov watched in horror as his master's body was lifted into the air and subjected to cuts and slashes from an unseen hand. Blood coated the walls and floor, and each strike caused Allenstein to groan in pain. Eventually, as quickly as the assault had begun, it ended. A bloodied and spent Allenstein dropped to the floor with a thick thud. Sakolov found him alive, but just barely.

"Our enemies are strong," Allenstein gasped to his lieutenant.

"Shall I call for a doctor?"

"No! Do not fear; I am not yet vanquished. We have lost *Kurit'*, but our mission remains unchanged. The Menagerie will be here and soon." With that, Allenstein rolled onto his side and demanded to be left alone. Sakolov did as he was told.

Back across the city, Bruhl and Lewis embraced in a warm gesture. Both men realized that they had survived an incredible experience. For Lewis, it was a revelation. He had learned first-hand, both as a sleeper and as a man wide awake, that evil—pure evil—was all too real.

"I think that your murders should cease now, Inspector Lewis," Bruhl said. Lewis smiled and nodded in agreement.

"I hope you are right. You and I will never be able to take credit for this one, for who would believe it?"

"Quite right. Let it disappear like smoke."

"That is the only way," Lewis said while hailing a rickshaw. "Are you going back to Peking?"

"Yes, but not right away. It rare for me to come this far south. Might as well enjoy it while I can."

"That is wise. One last thing, professor. Who do you think was controlling that....that...demon?"

"I do not know, and it is likely that we may never know. But, if you are curious, I suggest reading the obituaries and asking around among your fellow officers about any dead Europeans between now and tomorrow. Be on the lookout for anyone baring the tell-tale marks of a three-fingered attacker."

With that, Bruhl tipped his hat to Inspector Lewis and walked into the night. Lewis's rickshaw took him in the opposite direction. Both men went to bed that night believing that they had seen the last of the other.

Shanghai would surprise them once again.

THE SAAAMAAA RITUAL did banish Allenstein's familiar, but it did not stop the murders. The very next night after the strange events at Professor Bruhl's residence, Lewis and Sergeant Grant were called to the scene of yet another evisceration murder. Like the others before it, the victim was a transient Chinese national, and the body (or what was left of it) was found mutilated and partially eaten. At the chaotic crime scene, the detective heard the usual mumblings about fox spirits, the *huli jing*. Such talk was perfectly normal, for ancient Chinese custom asserted that the malevolent fox spirits frequently found the flesh of men delicious.

But, scattered among the usual superstitions, were other rumblings. Lewis heard them first and repeated them to Grant. The words dripped with menace. All Westerners in the city knew the words and what they meant, but usually the Chinese preferred to whisper them. The fact that some of the onlookers at the crime scene used them and loud enough hear made Lewis sweat.

"Do you see that group of men over there?" The sergeant nodded. "Tell them to come here." The burly Scotsman muscled his way through the crowd.

In stilted Mandarin, he demanded that a group of about four men, all youngish and dressed in Western clothes, come with him. Two outright refused and walked away before Grant could corral them. One played dumb and pantomimed that he did not speak Mandarin (or at least Grant's attempt at it). The final man cast his head low out of a small residue shame. He volunteered to go with Sergeant Grant.

"Why did you say, 'white ghost,' young man?" Lewis tried his best to intimate the lad, who gave off the aura of a university student.

"Because that is who is killing all these people. A white ghost. Like you and you," venom practically oozed out of his mouth as he said the words. Lewis saw the hatred in his eyes.

"Did you see the killer?"

"No, but all the elders know that it is true. A white devil is butchering this people so that he can eat their bones. It gives him great power."

"Has anyone seen this individual? Any idea where he may reside?"

The young man spat over his shoulder before answering. "I do not know. You would not arrest him anyway. If he is a Russian, maybe there will be justice. But if he's English like you," the man paused long enough to smirk, "SMP toadies will let him run free." The young man turned on his heels and made off before Lewis could respond.

"I don't like the sound of that at all," Grant said. "That was Boxer talk."

"Yes," Lewis responded, "or Bolshevik talk." Both men stared at each other with the knowledge that a planned demonstration by the Communist Party was scheduled for the following afternoon.

"That is all we need right now. A native uprising at the same time as a Bolshevik revolution with a bloody madman on the loose."

"I'll make sure to check in on the armory today," Grant said. "What about you?"

"I have to see a friend from Peking," Lewis added without further elucidation.

———

From the time of the body's discovery to the dawn of the next day, a series of monumental events took place in the city. None of them became known to Lewis or Bruhl until it was too late.

After dark, Allenstein and Sakolov left *Le Dagon Rouge* for the first time in weeks. The wounded Allenstein limped ahead of his lieutenant, his face a mask of determination. The men walked towards the Bund and its long harbor. Both maintained a healthy vigilance, for both assumed that the Special Branch had not given up their surveillance activities, even despite Agent Chow's death. Their goal that night was simple—rendezvous with their Green Gang contacts. The city's powerful crime outfit wanted to provide extra security, and get one last cut of Allenstein's substantial wealth, as the Russians made their final preparations. The Green Gang was oblivious to the truth behind that night's events; all they knew was what Sakolov had told them, which was that a massive shipment of guns and men was set to arrive from all across Europe.

The Russians found the warehouse abuzz with activity. Men, both European and Chinese, were busy unloading and opening wooden crates of all shapes and sizes. The boxes had labels from places as far afield as Greenland, Peru, and Maine. The already-opened inventory included an impressive array of weapons, which Sakolov began enumerating aloud.

"One hundred Colt .45 automatics. Two hundred Webley

revolvers, all chambered in .455. Sixty Colt .38 Detective Specials, plus twenty Police Positives. Twenty-five Thompson submachine guns, eighteen MP18s, and three Lewis guns. Rifles should include Springfields, Enfields, and Mausers.

There should also be one Maxim, water-cooled, affixed on the back of a Ford." Sakolov smiled when he came to the final item: several hand grenades of unique design. "And most important of are these, your gas bombs, Freiherr Allenstein."

Allenstein picked up some of the grenades and studied them. He looked at them like a proud father. Each one contained the black fever that Allenstein had discovered in San Francisco during his first exile. The unknown disease, whose origins were ancient when Lemuria was young, had the ability to paralyze Shanghai in perpetuity. This was Allenstein goal—to wash the city in an ocean of blood. The handful of Green Gang men smiled but had eyes that combined bewilderment with envy. They wanted the weapons but were suspicious of the foreigners. They especially disdained the half-clothed cultists who never strayed far from Allenstein. These were the men and women who had been butchering the vagabonds of Shanghai for months, but when in the presence of their master, they cowered like weak rabbits.

Hours went by until everything was unloaded from the ship that Allenstein had rented prior to arriving in Shanghai. Onboard, a few minutes past midnight, the captain, a tough old salt named Petersen, was surprised to see a man standing behind him.

"Well, that's everything, sir," the captain said to the silent man. When he did not respond, Petersen asked several questions, first in Russian then in his native Danish. He received nothing. The silent man glared at the captain for an uncomfortably long time, then, without warning, removed an automatic from his jacket and fired two rounds. Captain Petersen, a veteran of hard Atlantic storms and dangerous South Sea treks, was dead before his body hit the ground.

"What was that?" one of the Green Gang men asked in Mandarin. The alert gangsters unholstered their weapons and began looking around the entire warehouse.

"It was nothing," Allenstein said, "and it is of no concern to you anyway." The Russian growled something in an unknown tongue. The words caused all of the men from the ship to drop what they were doing and form up into neat and narrow lines. They moved with military precision, thus revealing who and what they were. Almost a decade after their exploits in the blood-soaked soil of Siberia, the remaining men of the Secret Army of Abraxas has reformed in Shanghai under their old commander.

Allenstein gave the men what sounded like orders. Again, the words were in a tongue unknown to anyone except the most ardent of magickal adepts. The Green Gang grew more and more anxious with each turn of the wizard's tongue. Allenstein's soldiers eventually dispersed and went back to opening the other crates.

"Settle down, men," Allenstein said to them. "You will not be sacrificed. You still have a role to play. Please help yourselves." Allenstein pointed to the newly unearthed weapons. The Green Gang men dived in with gusto. They were so focused on the guns and bombs and bullets that they did not pay any attention to the new items being brought up into the lights of the warehouse. The loyal men of the Secret Army of Abraxas cracked and pried open boxes and crates that contained strange idols—some carved in jade and obsidian, others in simple wood. Each idol was about the size of a statuette, although one figure took three men to stand aright.

This figure showed a type of monstrosity with membranous

bat wings, an octopus-like head, and tenacles where a mouth should have been. Even though the statute was made of ivory, one could still see the rubbery scales on the creature's arms and torso. The men of the Secret Army of Abraxas placed the smaller statuettes around the large statue in a pattern that vaguely resembled a kind of trapezoid. When they were complete, Sakolov removed from his pocket a new figurine and placed it at the end of the shape.

The figurine was the statuette of the Mi-Gul Shan that has been stolen from the study of Professor Bruhl. Once this was completed, Allenstein barked new commands. His soldiers and Sakolov quietly escorted the Green Gang gangsters out of the warehouse. Allenstein was left all alone with the unnatural idols and one final crate of goods. He opened the crate and removed from it a set of books. There were three books in total—one bound in human skin called the *Necronomicon*, one bound in black leather called the *Book of Eibon*, and a final tome called *De Vermis Mysteriis*. These were the books that Allenstein needed in order to get started with his mission, but to complete it he still needed the *Unaussprech-lichen Kulten*. Allenstein had a plan for the book's retrieval, but first he set about purifying himself. He stripped naked, thus revealing skin that was a patchwork of scars and hideous tattoos. Every part of his torso, arms, and legs were covered in reds, blues, greens, and purples. Some of the tattoos were representations of the very idols that he began to worship on that clear, dark night. Allenstein bowed his head and began chanting. He would not cease until the following night.

———

Elsewhere in the city, two Chinese men in tight white jackets stared at the strange foreigner. They mocked him in Mandarin.

"See, this is what happens when white ghosts drink too much," said one man to the other.

"You should talk; you drink like a white ghost yourself," said the other man. Both laughed and then went back to staring at the bound Westerner. One placed a bet about how long it would take before the foreigner died or killed himself in desperation. This was not an exaggeration; the unknown man had been locked away at the private sanitarium for months since being found wandering the streets in dirty rags that barely covered his body.

The SMP had arrested him for vagrancy, but after speaking with the man, who spoke English with an American accent, they decided that he was insane rather than a vagrant. They had delivered him to Dr. Benson's clinic, which the kindly old English gentleman had run since before the Boxer uprising. There, unknown to the outside world, the pitiful creature was allowed to waste away in a private room with his arms bound in a straitjacket. His only company were his thoughts and the two cruel-hearted Chinese orderlies.

"Make way, make way," said a third man. He arrived at the door with a metal cart carrying two serving trays. One contained porridge and the other a small selection of bread, butter, fruit, and onions. This was the patient's nightly meal. Alfred, the beefy orderly who had grown up in the cold mountains of Cumberland, pushed the two Chinese men aside and began delivering the food.

"C'mon now, you freak. You have to eat." Alfred gently pushed the trays through the small slot in the door. He expected the patient to grab the trays like he normally did, but instead he let the trays fall to the floor. The sight of spilled food made Alfred violently angry. He had grown up poor and underfed. His father would have lashed him for days for deliberately wasting food, and although it was against Dr. Benson's policy, Alfred planned on doing the same to the patient.

"Right then! Brace yourself." Alfred entered the room with his fists balled. He did not take a fighting stance because he did not expect the other man to fight back. Therefore, Alfred did not prepare himself for the headbutt that he received. He took one and then another. The blows caused blood to gush from his nose. The patient next kicked Alfred behind the knees. The orderly collapsed to the floor. The patient struck him several more times in the face and stomach until Alfred was silent and motionless. The man walked out of his cell and found that only one of the Chinese orderlies was left.

"Untie me," he said in halting Mandarin.

The frightened orderly did as he was told. He released the man from the straitjacket. Instead of a thank you, the orderly received two hard fists to the stomach. All of his mockery and jokes had caught up with him. He fell to the floor and moaned loudly as the man walked away into the night.

After so much suffering, Kenaghan was finally free again.

CHAPTER 9

APOCALYPSE IN SHANGHAI

INSPECTOR LEWIS WAS one of the few SMP officers not on demonstration duty that day. While the other officers were busy watching the red banners fluttering in the wind, Lewis was at his desk once again going over the facts of the Morrison case. It still did not make sense to him. Even Professor Bruhl, who had joined the inspector for tea, agreed that it was a confusing puzzle.

"And like you said, we may never know who sent that spirit thing," Lewis said to Bruhl.

"Yes. Experienced magicians often flee whenever one of their plans goes awry. I would wager that our friend has flown Shanghai already."

"You of course know that our murderer is someone else too. We kept finding bodies even after the ritual."

"Yes, I heard. A tragedy. It seems preposterous, but maybe everything that you have been dealing with is either unrelated or only tangentially related."

Lewis shook his head. "I cannot accept that, professor. There has to be a link somewhere. I will find it even if it kills me."

. . .

"I hope it doesn't. You are one of the best SMP officers, and one of the finest specimens of the Englishman abroad." Bruhl raised his mug of tea to Lewis. The policeman responded in kind.

"In a better world we'd be toasting sherry instead of oolong," Lewis said. Bruhl chuckled. The two men enjoyed the warm glow of good cheer until it was interrupted by the on-duty desk sergeant. The broad-shouldered Sikh barged in and wore an expression of deep fear.

"Sir. They have requested an all-hands at the demonstration. Things have taken a turn."

"What?!"

"They have deployed the Reserve Unit and the van, but they still need more men. The SVC is on high alert."

"Good Lord," Lewis said. "That will be all, sergeant." The Sikh saluted the inspector and returned to his post. Lewis retrieved his bullet-proof vest from behind his desk. He then placed his service-issued sidearm into his holster. He turned to Bruhl and told the gray-haired professor to go home and lock his doors.

"I'm afraid I have to disagree," Bruhl said. "I have seen battle before. And if this new battle is because of the Reds, then it would be my pleasure to have a go at them." Bruhl reached into his jacket and showed Lewis a revolver—an ancient but well-maintained Webley Bulldog. Lewis nodded.

"It's not much, but it will do. Just stick by me." Bruhl agreed and the two men made their way to the stationhouse's garage and helped themselves to one of the department's Fords. Within minutes they found themselves in the midst of a terrible firefight.

"Christ!" Lewis blasphemed as he swerved to avoid several rifles that were trained on the Ford. The crack of large-caliber bullets was heard at the same time as they hit the windshield and motor. Lewis grabbed Bruhl by the lapels and pulled him into the street. Both men took cover in an alleyway.

"Where did the Reds get that kind of firepower?" Lewis's question was drowned out by a cacophony of violence. Sounds of gunfire being exchanged back and forth cluttered the Shanghai sky. Lewis and Bruhl could hear men screaming in English, Russian, Japanese, Mandarin, and the myriad dialects of China. War had come to the city. Neither Lewis nor Bruhl knew it, but the war had started without warning.

Earlier that day, the massive demonstration of the Chinese Communist Party had wound its way through the various districts of the city. The Chinese authorities took a hands-off approach to the demonstration. Police officers merely stared, wide-eyed, as the sea of red flags and faces, both Chinese and Western, marched and chanted. Things changed once the demonstration neared the International Zone. Here, hundreds of SMP officers blocked off certain streets and stood ready for anything. These rough and hardy men kept their pistols, rifles, and shotguns at the ready. Sikh, Russian, Japanese, and British officers fully expected some kind of confrontation that day, for the Bolsheviks and the police had been adversaries for years in the city.

The Reds' main mission, as stated in the propaganda leaflets that were always scooped up by the SMP whenever they were found, was to rid the city of all "foreign devils." Shootouts between the Reds and SMP were not uncommon, and on certain nights of the year (May Day, for example), SMP men were told to keep off the streets. However, the crowd that greeted the SMP that day looked angry and hungry. Up front were the students, with their lean arms and aesthetic faces. Such types made up the majority of the Chinese Communist Party. But, in the back ranks stood men of a more menacing countenance. These men had the sharp, furtive faces of criminals and soldiers. Among them were a motley crew of members of the usually anti-Red Green Gang, Hui Muslim infantrymen paid to be there courtesy of looted Tsarist gold, and the dreaded Secret Army of Abraxas.

Allenstein's cultists marched as well, for there were ordered by their lord to spill and collect blood. None of these men were committed to the proletarian revolution. Instead, they had orders, all of which could be traced back to the dark mage Allenstein. It was on his command, which was given telepathically to Sakolov, that the apocalyptic siege of Shanghai began.

The SMP took direct fire from small arms without warning. The first volley hit several targets, including a killing blow that removed a veteran Japanese officer, Nakamura, permanently from service. The well-trained policemen took cover and unloaded with their .45s, .380s, and Enfields. The noise was overwhelming. The front ranks of the Reds broke loose and ran screaming into the Chinese part of the city. The Green Gang broke off early too after realizing that they had been tricked into an unwinnable battle with the authorities. The fighting was therefore left to the professionals: the SMP on one side and the strange mixture of Muslim and Russian occultists on the other.

Blood, guts, and brain matter littered the International Settlement. The SMP got the worst of it, for their opponents were veteran infantrymen who had fought long and vicious battles all across China and Siberia. Allenstein's veterans proved to be the better marksmen, but the Muslims outdid them in terms of sheer ferocity. One squad of short, squat Muslims rushed an isolated SMP officer firing blindly with a Thompson. They hacked him to pieces with their daggers. Parts of his white flesh were thrown high up into the air. His head, which was removed and held aloft, caused a ripple of vicious cheering to run through the crowd. The man's SMP compatriots responded in kind by pouring heavy fire down on the Muslims. Six were felled in a single volley.

Detective Robert Barry, a veteran of the 63rd (Royal Naval) Division, and Patrolman Gurn, an artilleryman during the Boer War, stood out in terms of mettle and spine. The two men, armed only with their pistols, killed an untold number of Muslim infantrymen by shooting and moving with deft speed.

The two men, one short and the other tall, were ghostly blurs in the gathering pink fog of cordite and blood. Yet, the true hero of the first melee was Patrolmen Sui. The elderly Chinese officer raced from the scene and found the nearest telephone. It was he who phoned the Reserve Unit. The riot officers joined the fray in record time. The sight of "the van," a hulking steel brute that had been designed after the horrors of 1919, inspired renewed confidence in the embattled SMP. The Reserve Unit used the van to drive a wedge into the enemy's ranks. The van became block designed to absorb rounds while the SMP let loose on their foes. For a time, it worked, and the Muslims fell like cut grass.

The men of the Secret Army of Abraxas proved to be quick thinkers, and they broke off the battle and fled deeper within the city. They knew that Shanghai, especially the Western-controlled areas, were honeycombed with narrow alleys and bystreets. They also knew that the SMP was wary of walking into those parts of the city under Chinese control. Accordingly, one half of the Russians began setting up ambush traps, while the others entered the Chinese zones and started sniping. This phase of the battle became a stalemate, with the SMP moving slowly through the International Settlement to liquidate the ambush positions and also avoid the accurate rifle and submachine gun fire coming from the Chinese zones. They also suffered harassment from wild-eyed and half-named men, many of whom attacked them with their bare hands. Dozens of SMP men, plus a smaller number of Allenstein's assassins, died during these small-scale skirmishes, which lasted until sundown.

As night descended the city, a strange figure began slinking its way through the many corpses left behind from the initial firefight. By that time, the SMP and two squadrons of the SVC (including one aerial unit observing everything from above), were too busy trying to put down the last of the Secret Army of Abraxas to notice.

However, the figure was observed by Inspector Lewis and Professor Bruhl, both of whom had suffered minor injuries that rendered them monetarily incapacitated with pain and blood loss.

"What in God's name is that man doing?" Lewis asked Bruhl. The Belgian remained quiet as he observed the man, or what looked like a man, as he went to each corpse and pressed something to their wounds. He and Lewis also watched in horror as the man used jars to scoop up blood from the bricks. These jars were then placed into a burlap sack and thrown over his shoulder. The man left as quietly has he had appeared.

"C'mon. Let's follow him," Lewis said while pulling on Bruhl's shoulder. The two wounded men limped along behind the shadowy figure as he wound his way through the labyrinthine streets of the city. They went deeper and deeper into the darkness, eventually reaching the banks of the Huangpu. Lewis and Bruhl saw the man enter a large warehouse on the riverfront. Here they paused and began discussing possible next moves.

"Could be a trap," Lewis said.

"Yes, it could. Then again, it is equally likely that he has yet to see us, and therefore is operating under the notion that he is all alone."

"Maybe," Lewis grunted. "What the devil could he want with all that blood?"

"My friend," Bruhl said solemnly, "something very, very wicked is afoot right now. Deploying a familiar is one thing but engaging in blood magick is quite another. And make no mistake, gathering up fresh blood like that can only mean black magick."

"So, it is our duty then, as Christian men, to do something about it."

"Quite right. Plus, I think are now close to solving your case."

"I pray that you are right," Lewis added.

"Yes. Prayer is what is needed." With that, Lewis and Bruhl limped towards the warehouse.

In one of the Chinese quarters of the city, two SMP officers, Janowski and Connors, raced after a lone Secret Army of Abraxas fighter. Janowski and Connors did not realize until it was too late that they had strayed into Chinese jurisdiction. All they cared about was removing their enemy from the earth. They chased him until all three came to a large and ancient wall that towered over all of them. The wall belonged to one of the old, half-forgotten fortifications of the Qing period. Realizing that he was trapped, the mad-eyed Russian turned and faced the two SMP officers.

"Drop your weapon," Connors shouted at him. The Russian remained stoic and refused to budge.

"Do it or we will shoot," Connors said. Janowski, an ethnic Pole who had grown up most of his life in Harbin, translated Connors's commands into Russian. Still, the other man remained silent. He reached into his jacket and removed a hand grenade. Before he could pull the pin, Connors and Janowski unloaded their .45 automatics into his chest. One of the bullets missed its mark and instead hit the grenade. This triggered the device, and instead of shrapnel, a cloud of black vapor engulfed the two SMP officers. The fetid smell of the vapor caused both men to collapse to their knees and vomit. Janowski cursed in Russian when he noticed through his tear-streaked eyes that his skin was bubbling. Connors did the same in English, but neither could stop their flesh from falling off their bones. Within seconds they were as dead as the Russian.

As if on signal, the remaining fighters of the Secret Army of Abraxas deployed their plague bombs as well. The combined releases created a large black cloud over the city, which spread the disease to all parts, Chinese and Western alike. Those unlucky enough to be outside felt their lungs fill up with vomit and their skin turn to soup. Waves of anguish could be hard in neighboring cities as hundreds died in the first ten minutes. After an hour, the local Japanese garrison and the US Marines of the 4th Regiment were sent into the city with gas masks. They too suffered from the dreaded and quick-acting illness.

Only one man in the entire city desired such death and destruction, for it had been his plan all along. And the plan was running perfectly right up until the moment when he was disturbed by Lewis and Bruhl.

"Fools!" Allenstein screamed at the top of his lungs. For the first time in over twenty-hours he had opened his eyes. The mad Russian saw in the dim light two pistols trained on him. Off to the side were his underlings, including a petrified Sakolov. Allenstein glared at Sakolov, which caused the criminal and long-time Red to rush head-first at Bruhl. He tackled the old professor and pinned the hand that held the Bulldog to the cold concrete floor.

Without saying a word, Lewis aimed his .380 and fired. The bullet entered Sakolov's forehead and exited through his neck. A thick thud was Sakolov's final addition to the world. Allenstein laughed in response.

"Save your bullets, gentlemen. You will need them. Not for me, but yourselves. You cannot stop what is coming and the horror of it all will consume you." The naked Allenstein stood up and walked towards Bruhl and Lewis.

"You were the ones who eliminated *Kurit'*. Well done. That was quite impressive, although ultimately futile. Another friend of mine found the book just tonight. It seems that it was in your possession, Inspector Lewis." Allenstein's words sent a chill through Lewis and Bruhl. From the shadows, the man that they had followed emerged into the dim light. He had the shape and size of a man, but his piebald skin, slanted eyes, and misshapen head gave him the appearance of a bipedal salamander.

"Mi-Gul Shan," Bruhl whispered.

"Impressive," Allenstein said. "He is not a full Mi-Gul Shan, but their blood courses through him. He is another pet for the Menagerie. Speaking of which..." Allenstein turned his head and looked at the salamander man. He said something in a strange tongue.

The creature, who once had been the adventurer Bergstrom, moved towards the arranged statuettes and statue and began coating them in blood. One by one each figure was covered in red except for the final statue. Allenstein pointed at Bruhl and Lewis.

"No need to go back out into the city, friend. You final contributors came to us." Bergstrom smiled and hissed. He removed two items from his burlap sack: a pistol and a book. He handed the book to Allenstein while leveling the gun at Lewis and Bruhl. Allenstein placed the book to his lips and kissed it.

"Von Junzt was a wise man. You must know that by now. But

you know who weren't wise? That bone-headed circle of men who tried to double-cross me. Morrison was the first. He thought he could bring me to Shanghai just to rob me. Idiot. I had Lucchini, that useless dago, Marsh, and Oppersdorff eliminate him on my behalf. If they had stayed the course, then they would still be alive today. All they had to do was focus on training my new army, but instead they too went rogue and generated plans to steal some gold—my gold. I took care of them, and now I will take care of you."

Lewis fired at Bergstrom and Allenstein. He hit both men, but the bullets did nothing. Both remained standing.

"Humans are such pitiful things. Fortunately, you will serve a higher purpose," Allenstein said. Bergstrom punctuated the threat by shooting Bruhl in the throat. The bullet made a nasty gash in the aged man's neck, and the blood poured out quick and fast. Lewis caught his friend before he could fall, and he tried his best to stop the bleeding. Bruhl looked into Lewis's eyes as the last traces of his life ebbed away.

"Bastard!" Lewis screamed once he saw that the professor was gone.

"Wrong. I have a father. Many in fact," Allenstein purred. Bergstrom grabbed handfuls of Bruhl's blood and painted the large statue of the god Cthulhu with it. Lewis was rendered frozen and helpless. He watched as the monstrosity at the center of the ritual became totally crimson.

"And now for the apex. Please enjoy the show." Allenstein turned his back to Lewis and his now empty pistol. He opened *Unaussprechlichen Kulten* and began reading aloud. Bergstrom prostrated himself before the idols and chanted alongside his master. His chants were sibilant hisses like a snake's. The noise harmed Lewis's ears, but he could do nothing to stop it. The chanting grew louder and louder, and the blood on the idols began disappearing, almost as entities inside of them were drinking it all up. This is what was happening, and Lewis let out panicked cries as he saw the idols transform from two- and three-dimensional representations into living horrors. The gods slowly emerged before him, causing Lewis to lose the last shreds of his sanity.

"The Menagerie, the Menagerie is here," Allenstein said with the passion of a zealot. "Come to me my gods. Come and worship ME!!!!" Allenstein lost all self-control and began running up to the creatures. He looked at them like his servants, which he fully believed that they were. The lesser deities, who had fully emerged into the human world whilst the great god Cthulhu took its time in reaching its bewildering heights, did not greet Allenstein warmly. The Mi-Gul Shan and others used their sharp teeth, claws, and weapons of indescribable character to hack and slash Allenstein until the powerful mage was nothing left but tattered flesh ribbons. Bergstrom saw all of this and tried to flee, but the deities similarly sliced him into multiple parts. The sounds were too awful to comprehend. The only living witness, Lewis, had fully lost his mind.

The deities turned their attentions to him as he saw the upper portions of Cthulhu come into view. The wings fluttered.

CHAPTER 10

THE HORROR ENDS

LEWIS WOULD NOT WAKE up again for weeks after that horrid night. His sanity, however, was never restored, nor did his memory ever come back to him. He did not know how he was rescued. He had no clue, nor did he ever learn, that Kenaghan was the man responsible for pulling him to safety that night after the bombing. The disheveled American had braved the fires and falling rubble to grab Lewis and pull him to safety.

Someone, most likely a member of the Green Gang, had managed to contact the Japanese garrison and inform them about the warehouse. The Japanese, operating under the knowledge that the warehouse contained that last Reds left alive in the city, bombed it from the sky. They flew multiple runs over the site and bombed it until the warehouse was nothing but dust. Nothing remained of it in the morning. All evidence of Allenstein and Bergstrom and their infernal designs were gone.

As for Lewis, he was first taken to a hospital in the International Settlement. There, the SMP's medical team diagnosed him as a helpless case. A month later he was placed on a transport ship that took him back to England.

· · ·

Lewis's minder wrote in his report that the inspector never said a word and mostly drooled during the voyage.

Less than a year after arriving in England, where he was taken in by his remaining relatives in Yorkshire, Lewis passed away from natural causes. He was buried in the local churchyard and was quickly forgotten.

Subsequent events in Shanghai made international news. The world's media and the League of Nations descended on the city. Peace was restored thanks to Japanese, American, British, and Chinese arms. The entire metropolis was sealed off from the world so that the remaining Bolsheviks and Red sympathizers could be arrested and sent away to a island prison in the Pacific. The truth was that this was mere cover for a more elaborate operation. The militaries of Europe, America, and Asia created a city-wide quarantine and detained all those who had been exposed to the black fever. Helping these people was deemed useless, so SMP officers, Chinese civilians, and Western expats afflicted with the strange virus were boarded onto ships and forced, at gunpoint, to leave the city. Two of the ships were sunk courtesy of Royal Navy submarines. Another batch of the afflicted became prisoners of the New Zealand authorities on the Territory of New Guinea. Here they were studied and worked until they all expired. Their corpses were burnt, and the ashes scattered across the South Seas.

One small batch of the afflicted were handed over to the Japanese authorities in Manchuria. The fate of these individuals would not be known until after the Second World War, when Soviet authorities uncovered the crimes of Unit 731.

As for Shanghai, the city made a surprising recovery after the horrific events. Both the Chinese and Western authorities forbade their populations from talking about the uprising or all of the weird incidents that happened during its duration. The city moved on, and by the time of the Japanese incursion in 1931, few bothered to think about it all.

All except for Kenaghan. The American decided to remain in the city as a vagabond. Like a ghost he wandered Shanghai and the surrounding cities until, in 1937, he was killed in a Japanese air raid. Thus, the final piece of the Shanghai Horror was laid to rest.